THE UNWANTED WEDDING

It was impossible for Honora to take her eyes from the Duke's, and as he saw the color creeping up her cheeks almost like the dawn creeping up the sky, he thought it was the most beautiful thing he had ever seen.

Then as her fingers tightened on his and he knew she was finding it hard to breathe he said:

"I love you, darling, but I have been afraid of telling you so in case I frightened you."

"I . . . I am not frightened," Honora said. "I love you! I did not . . . know that love could be . . . like this."

"What is it like?" the Duke asked, his lips very close to hers.

"It is part of the sunshine . . . music . . . the loveliness of the flowers and trees . . . and of course . . . the sky. . . ."

Then his lips touched hers and he knew that her softness, sweetness and innocence was something he had never imagined he would find. . . .

Bantam Books by Barbara Cartland
Ask your bookseller for the books you have missed

Barbara Cartland's Library of Love Series

The
Unwanted
Wedding

Barbara Cartland

BANTAM BOOKS
TORONTO · NEW YORK · LONDON · SYDNEY

THE UNWANTED WEDDING

A Bantam Book / April 1983

ISBN 0-553-23284-3

Published simultaneously in the United States and Canada

Bantam Books are published by Bantam Books, Inc. Its trade-
mark, consisting of the words "Bantam Books" and the por-
trayal of a rooster, is Registered in U.S. Patent and Trademark
Office and in other countries. Marca Registrada. Bantam
Books, Inc., 666 Fifth Avenue, New York, New York 10103.

PRINTED IN THE UNITED STATES OF AMERICA

O 0 9 8 7 6 5 4 3 2 1

Author's Note

*P*rince Albert remained a Coburger all his life. Nothing about him was English except his papers of Naturalisation. He looked German and spoke German to the Queen. Yet, in 1842 he felt convinced he was accepted in England.

At the same time, he never missed an opportunity to bring into the country "his own people." He started with Baron von Stockmar to help reorganise the Royal Household.

Both the Prince and the Queen were obsessed with the idea that marriage was a cure for all evils. When Prince Albert's brother Ernest became involved in a reprehensible love-affair, the Prince advised him to marry a virtuous wife and to "purify himself in the eyes of the world."

Ernest took the advice and married Alexandrina of Baden.

"Ernest's marriage," the Queen wrote, "is a *great, great delight* to us; thank God! I say, as I so ardently wished it."

Chapter One
1845

The candles in the Drawing-Room of Buckingham Palace did not glitter any more brightly than did the diamonds worn by the ladies who were dancing.

With their tiaras, necklaces, bracelets, and ear-rings they were a dazzling sight as they whirled round to the strains of a Viennese Waltz.

The Queen, despite the fact that she had had three children, was dancing energetically with a radiant look in her eyes which proclaimed her happiness.

Since her marriage to the staid, solemn, and pompous Prince Albert, who had captured her heart, she had not been able to indulge her love of dancing as much as she had before.

But tonight even he seemed to be affected by the gaiety of the music, which at times was hard to hear over the chatter of the guests.

Only one man seemed to look somewhat bored and cynical as he watched the rotating throng, and inevitably the eyes of almost every woman in the room kept returning to him.

The Duke of Tynemouth was not only so tall that it was impossible to overlook him in a crowd, but he was also extremely handsome and had an irresistible attraction

1

which resulted in his leaving a trail of broken hearts wherever he went.

Tonight, wearing the blue Order of the Garter across his chest and innumerable decorations, several of which were for outstanding gallantry, he certainly looked like a Prince if not a King as he performed his duties as Lord-in-Waiting to Her Majesty.

It was known that the Queen had a *penchant* for handsome men.

Just as at the time of her accession she had undoubtedly been infatuated with the handsome, alluring Lord Melbourne, it was thought by the gossips that despite her devotion to Prince Albert, she liked having the Duke constantly in attendance.

Tonight she even danced with him, which was a favour that did not pass unnoticed by the other Courtiers, although most of them were well aware that it was a doubtful pleasure where the Duke was concerned.

He disliked dancing, and the ladies who sought to captivate his vacillating affections could seldom persuade him to take the floor with them.

Now as the dance finished he moved to a corner of the Ball-Room and started talking to one of the Generals who was as usual complaining eloquently and at some length about the cuts in Army expenditures.

It was therefore quite a relief when he saw the Countess of Langstone coming towards them.

One of the most beautiful women in England, she had excelled her own reputation tonight by looking, the Duke thought, even lovelier than she usually did.

Her gown with its full skirt revealed her eighteen-inch waist, and her lace bertha embroidered with diamanté was almost exaggeratedly low to show the perfection of her white shoulders.

To make certain they were noticed, her necklace of enormous emeralds seemed to sparkle as mysteriously and alluringly as did her eyes.

As she stopped beside him, the Duke remembered how he had told her a few nights ago that she was like a tiger in the dark, and he thought it was a very apt simile for the fieriness of their love-making and the manner in which the Countess had hunted him.

He had avoided her for some time, not because he did not admire her. Indeed, it was impossible not to be aware that there was something magnetic about her, but he had no wish to become too involved with the wife of a man whom he met continually and, at the moment, almost every day at Buckingham Palace.

The Earl of Langstone was Lord Steward, and although the Duke found him somewhat of a bore and almost as dictatorial as Prince Albert, he had no wish to antagonise him.

But once the Countess had "set her sights" on a man she desired, it was difficult for him to avoid her, and because she was so persistent the Duke had eventually succumbed.

He certainly had no regrets at present, but he impressed upon Aline Langstone that they must be extremely circumspect.

He was well aware that with his reputation and her beauty it would be impossible for the gossips not to watch them like hawks.

"For goodness' sake, Aline," he had said to her last week, "do not speak to me except as distantly as possible when we are in public. Those gossiping women miss nothing!"

"I know that," Aline Langstone had answered petulantly. "They hate me, but if they do suspect that we mean anything to each other, I am not responsible."

"It does not matter whose the fault may be," the Duke said, "the result will be the same—they will somehow contrive to enlighten the Queen, and you know what she will feel about it."

"I know only too well!" Aline said sharply. "And George can be very jealous at times."

The Duke thought, as he had thought before, that it was a great mistake to have become involved with the Countess of Langstone. But now it was too late. He could not pull back, and if he was truthful he had no wish to do so.

He had never known a woman who was so insatiable and at the same time contrived to be alluring on each occasion in a thousand different ways.

He was amused and aroused and found himself beguiled by a new Circe when he had thought cynically that no woman was different from any other.

If he was intrigued with Aline Langstone, she, to her own consternation, was falling head-over-heels in love with him.

Never had she known such an ardent lover, and as she had quite a considerable experience, this was a very sincere compliment to pay him.

Actually, it was one the Duke had come to expect, and he often thought that other men must be extremely insensitive, or perhaps they were very selfish, that their wives never seemed before he met them to have any knowledge or appreciation of the Art of Love.

While he was not introspective about himself as a rule, he thought that perhaps it was because he gave the same thought to the women in his life as he gave to his horses.

He would never ride a horse without knowing everything about it, from its breeding to the personal preferences, dislikes, and tricks which every animal had.

With women it was basically the same, and while he amused himself, because each one was an individual he took the trouble to find out what aroused her, made her happy, and gave her the greatest satisfaction.

"I love you! I love you!" women had said to him a million times.

He knew that if they had not said so, he would have felt he had failed them.

Now he thought with a slight frown that it was indiscreet of Aline to speak to him at this moment in full view of everybody else in the Ball-Room.

She appeared indeed to be listening to the General, but he was aware that she was as palpitatingly conscious of him standing beside her as he was of her.

Then at last, like an Angel of Deliverance, an elderly lady came up to attract the General's attention.

"Sir Alexander, I have been looking for you," she said reproachfully. "You promised to take me down to supper, and if we do not go now, we may find it difficult to find a place."

"I can only apologise, my dear lady, if I have kept you waiting," the General replied gallantly.

He offered her his arm, and as they moved away the Countess turned quickly towards the Duke.

"I have to see you, Ulric."

He was about to tell her not to be so indiscreet, when something urgent in her voice made him ask:

"What is wrong?"

"I cannot tell you here, but come to tea tomorrow afternoon. I promise it is very important."

Now the Duke was definitely frowning.

He had made it a rule never to go to the Earl's house when he was in London, and it was in fact a rule he had made with all the women with whom he was involved.

It had saved him from a great deal of unpleasantness because invariably servants acted as spies for their Masters.

"I think it unwise," he said in a low voice.

"It is the only way we can meet, and I must see you! I have something to tell you which vitally concerns yourself."

The Duke looked at her in surprise.

Then, as if she felt that he had agreed to what she asked, she turned away to greet several friends who were just entering the Ball-Room.

For a moment the Duke wondered irritably what she had to tell him and why she had to be so dramatic about it.

Then he thought that the best thing he could do was not to go to the Langstones' house in Grosvenor Square and hope that what was so important for him to know could wait for another time.

He was aware, as the Countess was, that they would meet in a house-party at the weekend, and he knew that if they were clever it would be possible for them to find moments when they could talk without being overheard, and he could kiss her without being observed.

The Duke was quite used to women finding it impossible to wait even for a few days to see him, to be close to him, and for him to make love to them.

"How can I live another week without seeing you?" was a plaintive question to which he could often find no answer.

But because Aline had in fact been more or less circumspect in every way until now, he thought as he walked to another part of the Ball-Room that perhaps what she had to say to him was really of importance.

However, he remembered cynically how many times "something of importance" to a woman had been nothing but the aching desire to be in his arms and to feel his lips on hers.

Attractive though he found the beautiful Countess of Langstone, the Duke had no intention of causing an unnecessary scandal where she was concerned.

The Queen expected a very high standard of morality amongst those who served her in the Palace.

The Duke often thought drily that he had been born in the wrong period and would have found life far easier under Her Majesty's uncle George IV.

Then, indiscretions were habitual at the Palace, and anybody who appeared too discreet was looked at in surprise.

The Queen, however, had been exceedingly censorious of anything approaching immorality ever since she came to the throne as a young and innocent girl.

Now Prince Albert with his strict German conformity and Lutheran conscience had made things even more difficult than they had been for attractive men like the Duke.

"Dammit all!" one of the Duke's friends had said to him. "We might as well enter a Monastery and have done!"

"I hardly think that would solve any of your problems, Charles," the Duke had replied mockingly.

"At least I should not have Prince Albert breathing

down my neck and pontificating about the immorality of the country in a way which tells me all too clearly that he was really getting at me."

"Perhaps you are over-sensitive," the Duke had suggested.

"Nonsense!" his friend replied. "You know as well as I do that Germans are extremely intolerant of any human frailty, and the Prince is no exception."

The Duke knew this was more or less true.

The Prince was a true Coburger at heart. He might be shy and at times ill-at-ease, but he always behaved with a rigid dignity.

He had a lot of good qualities, but he lacked a sense of humour, and because he was over-serious and very respectable, the easy-going aristocrats, who often found their position at Court a bore, disliked him.

Looking round the Ball-Room, the Duke thought that with the beauty of the women and the elegance of the men who wore their clothes and their decorations in an unselfconscious manner, it was England at its best.

Yet he could, because he was extremely intelligent, understand why the Prince could not feel himself a part of it.

He also imparted his feelings to those near him so that it was he who always seemed the outsider in the Palace rather than the guests he was entertaining.

Quite suddenly the Duke wanted to yawn and go home.

Enough was enough, and although for a short while he could find the Royal Presence quite enjoyable, he knew there were always restrictions behind the laughter.

As far as he was concerned, tonight was not an evening he wished to repeat very often.

Then as she danced by in the arms of one of the *Aides-de-Camp,* Aline Langstone gave him a glance from under her long eye-lashes that he could not misinterpret.

For a moment he wondered if it had been parhaps too revealing.

Then as she turned her lovely face to laugh up at her partner, he was aware that no-one except himself would have seen it or, if they had, would have understood it.

She was certainly very attractive, and he was looking forward, as he had earlier in the day, to the weekend when they would be staying in the same house.

He was sure their hostess would contrive subtly, because she knew it was expected of her, that they should be together as much as possible.

Then he asked himself why he should wait for the weekend when Aline Langstone had already said that she particularly wished to see him tomorrow.

The Duke was sure it was a mistake to go to their house when the Earl was in London, and yet she had been so insistent that now he felt curious as to what she had to say to him.

Moreover, the glance she had just given him told him very clearly how much she wanted him and that the fires he had ignited in her were still blazing.

"I shall do as she asks," the Duke decided.

He walked from the Ball-Room with a smile on his lips.

* * *

The following afternoon, the Countess of Langstone was waiting in the long L-shaped Drawing-Room at Langstone House in Grosvenor Square.

It was not a particularly attractive building, having been in the family for nearly fifty years without having many modern improvements made to it.

At the same time, the Reception-Rooms were impressive and beautifully decorated with a profusion of flowers.

The Countess was well aware that the high windows with their draped velvet and tasselled curtains and the gilt-decorated French furniture made a fitting frame for her beauty.

She had of course been painted by several distinguished artists, but of the portraits hung in her husband's house in London and his mansion in the country, including one particular painting which decorated his bedroom, none of them did her justice.

The artists had portrayed very faithfully the whiteness of her skin, the darkness of her hair with blue lights in it, and the perfection of her features.

But they had none of them quite managed to capture the enticement of her lips or the irresistible invitation in her eyes.

Now as she moved about the Drawing-Room she was reflected in several gilt-framed mirrors, and as she glanced at herself she was well aware of the grace with which she moved and the sinuous length of her long neck.

Long necks, small waists, and well-curved figures were most admired in the beauties of the day, and while the Queen was too short to qualify, the Countess won on every point, as the Duke had told her.

"How can I lose him?" Aline Langstone asked herself now as she waited for him to arrive.

Ever since she had first burst into the Social World on the arm of the very eligible and very important Earl of Langstone, she had been admired and acclaimed in a manner which would have turned any young girl's head.

Aline had been no exception.

But while she flirted and certainly encouraged every man she met to compliment her as eloquently as he was capable of doing, she had been faithful to her husband until she had presented him with two sons.

After that, having done her duty, she had melted into the arms of one man after another, managing to conceal her behaviour from the Earl only because he believed her to be a cold woman.

He had certainly been unable to light the fires within her that flickered enjoyably with several lovers before they burst into a blaze for the Duke.

From the very first moment she had seen him, standing out amongst a number of other good-looking and well-dressed men, she had been determined to ensnare him.

He had been more elusive than she had expected, but she was confident that she would succeed.

When eventually she had captured the Duke, she had learnt that her instinct had been right in telling her he was different from any other man.

A number of other women had thought the same thing, but to Aline the Duke was a revelation.

Only by holding on tightly to her commonsense had she prevented herself from falling so desperately in love as to throw away all restrictions and precautions.

"Oh, Ulric," she had said to him the last time they were together, "why could I not have met you when I was young, before I married George?"

"If you had, I doubt if I should have noticed you," the Duke had replied. "I find young girls a crashing bore."

"That is not the right answer," Aline complained. "I was not as beautiful as I am now, but I was still lovely enough to make George swear the moment he saw me that I should be his wife. It was the only time he has ever been positive about love."

The Duke did not bother to argue.

He only thought, as he had dozens of times before, that he had no intention of marrying if he could possibly avoid it.

Although he was prepared to make love to another man's wife and to make a fool of her husband, it still made him feel a little uncomfortable when she disparaged the man she had married.

He knew that if that ever happened to him, it was something he would never forgive, and he would undoubtedly defend his honour and his family name by killing the man who had cuckolded him.

Duels were forbidden both by the Queen and by law, but those who were too chicken-hearted to meet each other at dawn in Hyde Park crossed the Channel to shoot at each other in Calais or Boulogne.

Whichever why it was done, the Duke thought it was a messy business, and the easiest way to avoid such a confrontation was not to be married.

He himself was a very good shot and extremely quick with a pistol. He knew that any husband who suspected him of seducing his wife would think twice before he challenged him.

He himself would not hesitate for one moment, but as quite certainly he would be the victor, it would be unsporting to find himself in such a position.

"I shall never marry," he often said to his friends.

"Do not be so ridiculous!" was the reply. "You know you have to produce an heir."

"There is no hurry for that," the Duke replied.

Now at thirty-three he had still managed to remain a bachelor, despite the fact that ambitious parents who had marriageable daughters plied him with invitations.

While the girls themselves looked at him with wistful eyes, as they did so they were aware that he had no idea they even existed.

The type of woman with whom the Duke spent his time and who captured his interest was always very sophisticated, witty, and at the same time extremely feminine.

He liked women with soft voices and soft bodies.

He had never found himself interested in women with sharp tongues, and, perhaps because he was almost aggressively masculine himself, he preferred them to be small and fragile.

"I presume it brings out the protective instinct in you," a man had said to him mockingly.

The Duke had smiled cynically since he was well aware that most of the women with whom he associated did not need protecting and were in fact very capable of looking after themselves.

At the same time, he knew that they looked up to him and accepted his domination, and that no woman had yet ever wanted him to be anything but masterful both to her and to everybody else.

* * *

The following morning after the party at Buckingham Palace, the Duke rose early as he always did and rode in the Park.

There were far more men riders than women, and he wondered if it would have been easier for Aline to have met him there to tell him her secret, if that was what it was.

Then he remembered that she would not ride alone, as it would be inconceivable for her to appear without her husband or a groom in attendance.

After breakfast in his house in Park Lane, the Duke

dealt with a number of letters that his secretary had for him to sign.

He then attended a meeting of the Masters of Fox-hounds, which was taking place in the house of the Duke of Beaufort.

This kept him busy until luncheon-time, and then instead of returning home he ate at White's Club and listened to the latest gossip of its members, who always had something to impart which no-one else had heard of before.

The Duke received several invitations for different ways to spend his afternoon.

But because he knew he would have to be at Langstone House at half-past four, he went to Lord's Cricket Ground to sit in the Pavilion and watch a game of cricket before finally he drove to Grosvenor Square.

He arrived at Langstone House only ten minutes later than he knew Aline would be expecting him.

The Countess had been pacing the room wondering frantically whether he would turn her down because what she wanted was against his principles, or rather one of the rules he made for himself.

One thing about the Duke which women always found infuriating was that they could never be sure that he would do what was expected of him.

He was a law unto himself when it came to his own interests.

Aline Langstone knew that if he chose to think it was a mistake for her to invite him to tea, he would not hesitate to leave her waiting for him while he did something else, without making any explanation.

When she thought of how other men crawled on their knees for her favours, she found this an exasperating trait in the Duke.

And yet, regrettably, it made her love him all the more.

She knew that however angry she might be, he would only have to touch her for her to melt into his arms and find her heart beating against his so that it would be impossible to think of anything but her need of him as a man.

"Heavens knows why he is different from every other man I have ever met!" she exclaimed.

She stopped in front of one of the mirrors to look at her reflection, and she knew that without doubt she was the loveliest woman in the whole of the Social World.

It was a gift for which she was always extremely grateful, and because she was so beautiful she was sure she could hold the affection of any man for just as long as she wanted him.

With, of course, the exception of the Duke.

She always had the uncomfortable feeling when he left her even after hours of passionate love-making that she might never see him again.

It made her want to hold on to him with both hands and make him swear that what he felt for her was a love that was eternal and would never fade.

But she was astute enough to know that this was the last way of holding him, and that only by letting him think he was free would she keep him her prisoner.

Her long experience of men should, Aline thought, have made her know exactly how to handle the Duke.

Yet, because he was unlike any other man who had ever been her lover, she knew that if he wished to leave her he would do so and no amount of pleading or tears would persuade him to stay.

"Of course he loves me, I know he loves me," she told her reflection.

But while her voice spoke positively, in her eyes there was a question to which she had no answer.

Suddenly the door behind her opened, and she turned sharply as the Butler said:

"His Grace the Duke of Tynemouth, M'Lady!"

"What a lovely surprise!" Aline managed to exclaim as she moved towards the Duke, holding out her hand.

"We will not wait for my other guests, Dalton," she said to the Butler. "They may be late, so bring the tea."

"Very good, M'Lady."

As the door shut, the Duke raised Aline's hand to his lips to ask with a twinkle in his eyes:

"Who else is expected?"

"Oh, quite a number of friends," she replied airily.

"You are a liar, but a very beautiful one," he retorted, "and of course I am waiting to hear why it was so important for me to come to see you this afternoon."

"Come and sit down."

Aline seated herself on a brocade sofa with flowers arranged behind it so that they made a perfect background for her beauty, while he took a chair opposite her.

He waited until the servants had brought in a large and elaborate tea, and as the door closed, Aline, making no pretence of touching the tea-pot, bent forward to say in a low voice:

"I had to see you and there was no other way I could do so."

"Why it is so urgent?" the Duke asked. "We are meeting each other at the weekend."

"I know," Aline replied, "and I am looking forward to it more than I can possibly say. But, darling, something terrible has happened that you must know now—at once!"

Because there was such a note of urgency in her voice, he said sharply:

"Then tell me what it is!"

The Countess drew in her breath.

"The Queen has decided that you shall marry the Princess Sophie of Saxe-Coburg-Gotha!"

As she spoke, the Duke stiffened.

Then he stared at her as if he thought he could not have heard her a-right.

"What are you saying? How do you know this?" he asked at length.

"The Prince told George yesterday morning, and of course he has arranged it as she is his cousin."

"Are you absolutely sure that is what he said?"

"You know George never exaggerates, and of course he was delighted. As I have told you before, he suspects that we are seeing too much of each other."

The Duke rose to his feet to stand holding on to the mantelpiece and looking down at the fire.

He was seeing not the flames flickering over the coals but the fat, plain face of Princess Sophie, whom he had met a month ago at Buckingham Palace.

She had come to England at the invitation of the Prince, and the Queen, to please her adored Albert, had made a great fuss of her.

The Duke had actually met the Princess on several occasions and had thought her a typically dull, dowdy German *Fraulein* who would grow even duller and uglier when she was a German *Frau*.

She was already too fat and too red-faced, and her clothes accentuated all the worst points of her body, just as the way she did her hair brought out the worst features of her face.

He could imagine no worse fate than being married to the Princess, and since German families, especially the Saxe-Coburgs, clung to one another like leeches, he would be permanently entertaining her even duller and uglier relations.

He was silent for so long that at last Aline asked in what was little above a whisper:

"What are you going to do?"

The Duke turned round.

"That is just what I am wondering. What the hell can I do expect refuse point-blank to contemplate such a life of unmitigated hell?"

"I guessed that was how you would feel! Oh, Ulric, it is terrifying for you, but somehow you must be clever about it."

She was silent for a moment before she added:

"That was why I thought you had to know at once, before the Prince or the Queen tell you what they have in mind."

"What has happened so far?" the Duke asked. "How far has this absurd idea progressed?"

"I think, from what George told me," the Countess replied, "that after they had stayed here the Princess, or perhaps it was her father, wrote to Prince Albert and said how happy they had been in England. They also insinuated that the Princess would like to marry an Englishman."

She looked up at the Duke's scowling face apprehensively before she added:

"George thought that Prince Albert had said she had actually named you as the type of Englishman to whom she would like to be married."

"She may want to marry me," the Duke exclaimed furiously, "but I am damned if I will marry her!"

"Darling, if the Queen decrees it, you will have to."

"This is supposed to be a free country and a democracy!"

"Not where the Queen is concerned, and you know if she is determined, the Prince has an obstinacy which is very German."

The Duke knew this was true.

At the same time, the Queen could, if she wished, be extremely dictatorial, even towards the husband she admired.

It flashed through the Duke's mind that the Queen always got her own way.

The Duke had always been told that when the Prince had become her husband he had assumed he would have a say in the choice of his own Household.

But the Queen did not agree.

She had chosen the gentlemen who were to be closest to him, and when he had wanted a German as his private secretary, the Queen had been absolutely adamant.

In fact, she had already chosen young Mr. Anson, and that he actually became a close friend of the Prince was just a matter of luck.

No-one could be constantly at Buckingham Palace without being aware that the Queen when she became "Royal" was quite prepared to be not only a Ruler but at times a tyrant.

Although as a Duke he might be omnipotent in his own particular sphere, he had the uncomfortable feeling that if he came up against the Queen on a subject on which she had set her heart, he would be the loser.

To be married to the Princess Sophie was so unthinkable that he could hardly believe that Aline was not making up the whole idea.

However, he supposed it was something he might have anticipated would happen, although it had indeed never entered his mind.

To begin with, as his father's son he was not only one of the most important and certainly the wealthiest Duke in the United Kingdom, but his grandmother on his mother's side had been related to the Royal Family.

He would therefore be acceptable as the husband of a minor Royalty and in this case a Princess who was not only of Royal Blood but related to the husband of the Queen of England.

As he thought of her plain face and the platitudes she had mouthed when he had talked with her, he could only fling himself down in the chair he had just vacated and ask despairingly:

"Having told me of the horror that is encroaching upon me, have you any idea what I can do about it?"

He did not wait for Aline to reply but added:

"Other than to go abroad and stay there!"

She gave a little cry.

"Oh, Ulric, you cannot do that! I cannot lose you! That is why I have been thinking that there is just one possible way out of this."

"I should certainly be interested to hear it."

"It may sound a little crazy," she went on, "but I have thought and thought about it. The only way I can think of in which you could avoid Princess Sophie and having to spend months of the year travelling backwards and forwards to Saxe-Coburg is for you to be married to somebody else!"

The Duke looked at the Countess as if she had taken leave of her senses.

"Did you say—married?"

"Yes, darling, and as I say, it may seem mad. But surely to be married to an ordinary English girl who is young, pleasant, complacent, and ready to do what you wish

would be better than having all those Royals sitting on top
of you."

"I have no wish to marry Princess Sophie or anybody
else," the Duke said.

"I know that," Aline agreed, "but it would be much
worse to be married to her and have Prince Albert lectur-
ing you from morning to night than it would be to choose
your own wife."

There was a certain amount of twisted logic in this, the
Duke thought, and after a moment's silence he said somewhat grudgingly:

"I suppose even to be engaged might prevent them
from ordering me to marry the Princess."

"Exactly!" Aline said. "And although I cannot bear to
think about it, you have to be married sometime."

"But not for many years."

"But you cannot afford to wait for years, the Queen will
see to that."

There was silence until the Duke said disagreeably:

"Well, whom do you suggest I should marry? Before
you suggest again 'a young girl,' I do not know any."

"I am aware of that," Aline answered, "and besides,
there is no time for you to go wooing one. Your engagement, if you are to be saved from the Princess, will have
to be announced immediately."

"Can I not invent some woman I have never seen and
who does not actually exist?" the Duke asked hopefully.

"No, of course not!" Aline replied. "But I have somebody in mind whom you can marry, and there will be no
difficulty in announcing your engagement the day after
tomorrow."

There was silence before the Duke said:

"I suppose I am being rather obtuse, but I cannot see
quite how you come into this, Aline, or why you are so
interested."

"Can you really ask such foolish questions?" she enquired.
"I love you, Ulric, you know that I love you, and I will do
anything to prevent us from losing the happiness we have
found together."

Her voice sharpened as she finished:

"You know as well as I do that if you marry the Princess we shall never have another chance of being alone together."

She gave a groan as she said:

"You have been at Buckingham Palace long enough to know that the Queen is aware of everything that concerns her Household, and I expect too she knows about us, however discreet we have been! But if you were actually one of the family, they would keep you so occupied that you would never have a free moment to yourself."

The Duke knew this was true, but as there was no point in merely agreeing with Aline, he said nothing.

"I have been thinking," the Countess continued, "ever since George told me what was going to happen, that if you married somebody completely outside the Royal Circle, then it would be impossible for the Queen to interfere between you and me."

She paused before she added:

"Actually, the girl I have in mind will make it even easier for us to be together than it is now."

"'The girl you have in mind'?" the Duke repeated sharply. "What girl? Who is she?"

"That is what I am going to tell you. But do not look so cross! This is the only possible way I feel I can save you."

As she spoke, the Countess rose from the sofa and crossed to the chair in which the Duke was sitting.

She knelt down beside him, turning her beautiful face up to his as she said:

"I love you! I love you! Oh, Ulric, I cannot lose you! That is what will happen if the Queen and the Prince have their way."

She was not able to finish the sentence.

The Duke bent forward to put his arms round her, and now his lips were on hers, kissing her passionately, demandingly, and, because he was upset, almost brutally.

The fire that was never far from the surface in either of them leapt into a blaze.

As their kisses became more insistent, the Duke lifted her until she was lying in his arms, and she could feel his heart beating as frantically as her own.

The sound of a coal falling in the grate made them both aware of the risk they were running.

In a choked little voice, because she found it hard to breathe, Aline managed to say when the Duke raised his head:

"We must be sensible . . . but it is very . . . difficult when you . . . kiss me like . . . that."

"I want you!" he said. "It is damnable that we have to wait until the weekend!"

"I know, but there is a great . . . deal you have to . . . do before . . . then."

It was still difficult for her to speak in anything but a gasp, but she extricated herself from his arms and with an effort moved back to the sofa on which she had been sitting.

As she did so, she put her fingers up on either side of her forehead, aware that he was watching her every movement and knowing she was very graceful.

"I am trying to think," she said, "and, darling, you must not prevent me from telling you what I have in mind, because when you kiss me I can think of nothing but you."

"I want to kiss you," the Duke said.

As he spoke he had a vision of the Princess Sophie's fat, emotionless face, and he knew that anything, however unpleasant or outrageous, would be better than having to marry her.

"It almost seems as if fate is playing into our hands," Aline began, "because tomorrow—actually it was against my will—George's niece arrives here from Florence."

"His niece?" the Duke asked almost automatically.

He was thinking not of what he was saying but of how much the woman opposite attracted him.

She had aroused him, as she always managed to do, to a state where he felt that nothing else was important except that he should make love to her.

"Her name," the Countess was saying, "is Honora. I do not suppose you remember meeting George's brother. He was very popular, and although he was wildly extravagant he had a great many friends. Unfortunately, he was killed in an accident while out hunting."

"I seem to remember hearing about it," the Duke replied vaguely.

"His wife had died previously," Aline went on, "and of course, as poor Harry left no money and a mountain of debts, George had to pay up as well as look after his daughter. She was sixteen and, as I remember, quite a pretty little thing."

"What happened to her?" the Duke asked in a voice which showed he was not particularly interested.

"As I had neither the time nor the inclination to look after a girl of sixteen," Aline said, and now there was a sharp note in her voice, "I persuaded George to send her to a very good Finishing-School in Florence."

The Duke did not speak as she went on:

"As she is now over eighteen, they have refused to keep her any longer, and she is arriving here tomorrow."

There was silence. Then the Duke said:

"Are you seriously suggesting that I should marry this girl?"

"It seems a reasonable idea."

"Reasonable?"

"But, darling, what alternative is there except to marry the Princess? George will make no objections to your marrying Honora, nor shall I, and the engagement can be announced immediately."

"How can I marry a girl who is just out of the School-Room and who has not the slightest idea of the life I lead or what will be expected of her?"

The Countess smiled.

"Is that not rather a good thing? Do not be so stupid, Ulric. Can you not see that as she knows nothing about Society life, or about us, we can do just exactly as we like. Once you are married to her, she can stay in the country with your children! You must have at least half-a-dozen! And you will be as free as you are now!"

The Duke stared at her.

"I think this is the craziest idea I have ever heard!"

Aline made a very pretty gesture of helplessness before she said:

"I was only trying to help. Perhaps you would prefer to discuss it with the Queen!"

The Duke groaned.

"You know I cannot do that!"

"When are you next going to Buckingham Palace?"

"I am in attendance on Thursday."

"Then how do you know Her Majesty is not going to speak to you then? Once she has actually informed you that she will give the Royal approval and her blessing to your marriage with Prince Albert's delightful and charming cousin Princess Sophie, how can you refuse?"

The Duke was silent, knowing, infuriating though it was, that Aline was speaking the truth.

It would be impossible for any one of the Queen's Household to refuse what she and Prince Albert would think was a most gracious gesture on their part without being ostracised from the Royal Presence and being deprived of his official duties.

He was well aware that the Queen could, as her Ladies-in-Waiting knew only too well if they put a foot wrong, expel anyone from Court for six months at a time, or, if the crime was a serious one, more or less exile them for life.

"There must be another way out," he remarked aloud.

"If there is, I cannot think of it."

There was a long silence before he said:

"You say this girl is arriving tomorrow. Suppose she refuses to marry me?"

Aline laughed.

"Is it likely she will do that? Besides, George and I will tell her how extremely fortunate she is, and as she has no money, she must either do as we say or starve!"

"When it comes to getting your own way, I do not think there is much to choose between you and the Queen!"

"You must just ask yourself which you prefer as a *close* relationship."

Aline accentuated the word "close," and as she looked

at the Duke and their eyes met, they were both aware
what the other was feeling.

"You do see, dearest," she said in little more than a
whisper, "that it would be so easy for us to see each other,
and even George would be unable to prevent it."

She paused before she added:

"We could stay for weekends at each other's houses, and
as Honora has no other friends in London, she will
obviously want us to be continually with you at Tynemouth
House."

"That is the one good idea in the whole 'box of tricks'!"
the Duke said savagely.

"And a very important one," Aline added softly.

The Duke rose to his feet and she wondered if he was
about to leave.

But he walked across the room and locked the door,
then put his hands out and pulled her from the sofa into
his arms.

He was kissing her again, kissing her until it was
impossible to be aware of anything but the fire burning
through them both with a rising desire that was both a
pleasure and a pain.

Only as they clung closer and closer did the Duke think
vaguely at the back of his mind that he was paying a very
high price for the loss of his freedom.

Chapter Two

*H*onora, arriving in London with three other girls from her School and a Nun in attendance, felt herself growing more and more apprehensive.

Having been away for over two years in Florence with little contact with her uncle and aunt, she was intelligent enough to realise that they had no particular wish for her to return to England.

In fact, she had written the previous year saying that now that she was approaching eighteen, the School did not wish her to stay.

The only reply was a letter from her uncle's secretary to say that they were communicating with the Mother Superior to the effect that she was to remain there for another two terms.

It had been embarrassing not only to be the oldest girl in the School but also to be the cleverest.

She had actually gone to the Mother Superior and suggested that as she was so much older than the other girls, perhaps it would be best if her work was not considered in the award of prizes.

"That is very unselfish of you, Honora," the Mother Superior answered, "but we really cannot alter the rules of the School just for one person who should have left by now."

"I know that, Reverend Mother," Honora replied, "but what am I to do? My aunt, who is very beautiful and still quite young, has no wish to chaperone me, and I have no other relatives who would wish me to live with them."

24

The Reverend Mother's eyes softened, for she realised only too well why the Countess of Langstone, who was an acknowledged Social Beauty, did not want her niece.

Another woman, even if only slightly attractive, would be a rival.

But in fact Honora in the last two years had grown and developed until she had, the Reverend Mother thought, not only a very lovely face but also a character to match it.

There was nobody in the School who was a better influence or whom the younger girls admired more.

The Mother Superior knew that if Honora was her daughter she would be very worried at her being plunged straight from the quiet security of the Convent into the Social Circle of which her aunt was the leader.

At the same time, everybody knew that the Queen of England and her husband, Prince Albert, were a model couple who were an example of all that was best and finest in married life.

The Reverend Mother found herself praying that Honora, whom she had grown to love, would marry a decent man and not anybody with a reputation like those of the Queen's uncles who had scandalised all Europe.

Aloud she said:

"I know, Honora, that wherever you go, whatever you do, you will remember what we have taught you here and follow the dictates of your conscience."

"I will try, Reverend Mother," Honora replied.

The other girls, who had gone home in the holidays to Paris, Rome, Madrid, and other gay cities, were very voluble about the parties, Balls, and Receptions which their parents gave.

They also whispered about handsome young men who paid them attention even though they were still at School.

'I am so ignorant about such things!' Honora thought helplessly.

She hoped, although she thought it unlikely, that her aunt would help her and instruct her as her mother would have done.

'If only Papa were alive,' she thought wistfully as she

travelled across France, remembering how dashing he had been and how he had laughed at everything, even his debts.

"Something will turn up," he would say loftily when tradesmen were pressing him and he would wonder where his next penny was coming from.

"That is a gambler's outlook, Papa," she said to him once.

Harry Lang laughed before he replied:

"All life is a gamble. Sometimes you are up and sometimes you are down, and the only thing to do is to take it all philosophically and believe that eventually, whatever the odds against you—you will win!"

Because his gaiety was infectious, Honora realised there was no point in arguing with him.

It was easier to laugh as he did and hope that the right cards would turn up the next time he played.

But when he was killed in the hunting-field during, as one of his friends had said, one of the best runs they had had that Season, neither cards nor horses had shown a win for some time.

Honora had therefore been very conscious of the large amount of debts that her uncle had to pay on her father's behalf, and her Aunt Aline had made sure she did not forget it.

"I hope you are grateful," she had said sharply when she informed Honora that she was to go to Florence.

"Thank you very much, Aunt Aline," Honora murmured.

"It is costing your uncle a great deal of money to have you educated in the smartest and naturally the most expensive Finishing-School in Europe. I suppose you know what that word entails?"

Because Honora was well read, for her mother had seen to that, she was aware that girls from aristocratic families in France and Italy had for generations been sent to what were now called "Finishing-Schools."

Not only did the pupils have Academic lessons, but it was also made sure that before they entered the Social

World they were proficient in the art of being a successful woman.

This meant that the curriculum included painting, learning French, German, and Italian, playing the pianoforte, riding, and, most important of all, dancing.

As was traditional, Nuns ran the School, but the majority of the teachers came in from outside and were exceptionally gifted.

Once Honora got over being homesick and feeling the loss of her father, her lessons filled her whole life, and she enjoyed the classes, realising she was improving her brain with everything she was taught.

It was her father who had said to her on more than one occasion:

"For Heaven's sake, make sure, dearest, that you have something to talk about besides yourself. A pretty face is a good introduction, but a man quickly grows bored with lips, however irresistible, that can only mouth platitudes."

Honora had laughed as he had meant her to do, but at the same time she knew that he was speaking seriously.

After her mother had died there were a number of beautiful women anxious to console her father, and she had studied them with interest.

She was not, which was unusual, jealous of them as many young girls were jealous, because she knew she held an unassailable position in his heart which no-one else could touch.

"Hurry and grow up, poppet," her father had said, "and then we can have a great deal of fun together. But let me tell you, I shall be a very strict Chaperone! I have no intention of allowing you to be pursued by the wrong sort of man."

"What is the wrong sort of man, Papa?"

Harry Lang had thought for a few seconds before he said:

"I suppose, if I were not your father, that would apply to me!"

"Oh, no, Papa!"

"It is true. You must avoid men who are out for amusement and not marriage, and men who marry a woman because she has money or a grand social position."

"Nobody is likely to marry me for either of those two reasons," Honora pointed out.

"No, my dearest, but while they will be beguiled and enchanted by your face, you must make sure they want more than that."

Honora looked puzzled, and he explained:

"A man must love you for your real self, your personality and your character, as I loved your mother. She was not only the most beautiful person I have ever seen, but the sweetest and the most adorable."

There was a note in her father's voice which told Honora only too clearly how much he missed his wife.

Then he said:

"I loved her and—this is the truth—we never for one moment grew bored with each other, because we laughed at the same things and stimulated each other's minds. And that, my poppet, is very, very important when you are choosing a husband."

"But suppose the man with whom I fall in love does not want to marry me?" Honora asked.

"He will," her father replied, "but do not fall into his arms too quickly like an over-ripe peach. Give him a run for his money and he will appreciate you all the more when he catches you."

Honora had understood exactly what her father was saying.

When she watched the lovely women fluttering round him because he was so handsome, and attempting to entice him by wiles that were so obvious, she felt they were not only embarrassing but foolish.

She could understand why he laughed at them and how, if he seemed infatuated, it never appeared to last for long.

"Are you bored with Lady Studleigh?" she remembered asking her father when she was only thirteen.

She thought he hesitated before he replied:

"You have asked me a direct question, my dearest, and

so I will give you a direct answer—yes! She is a bore and I have no further wish to be bothered by her."

Because the servants talked, Honora was aware that Lady Studleigh's groom called almost every day with notes which smelt of her perfume but which after a while her father did not even bother to open.

Once when he was out she had come to the house and walked into the Drawing-Room where Honora was sitting reading.

"Where is your father?" she demanded.

Honora, who had not heard her enter the room because she had been concentrating on her book, jumped to her feet to curtsey and say:

"I am sorry, Lady Studleigh, I did not hear you arrive."

"I asked you where your father was. I want to see him!"

There was no doubt that Lady Studleigh was looking very beautiful.

She was wearing a fashionable bonnet and her red hair gleamed beneath it, and her green silk pelisse in the very latest fashion was very becoming.

Her skin was very white, her eyes had a touch of green in them, and it flashed through Honora's mind that it was very strange that her father could have become bored with her so quickly.

Aloud she said:

"I am afraid Papa is out."

"He is always out when I want to see him," Lady Studleigh said. "When will he be back?"

"I do not know," Honora replied. "I think he has driven down to Ranelagh."

"He will not be doing that alone!" Lady Studleigh exclaimed sharply.

Suddenly she sat down on a chair and said in a very different tone:

"What am I to do? Oh, God, what am I to do?"

Feeling shy and awkward, Honora did not know how to reply.

She only watched Lady Studleigh's beautiful eyes fill with tears. Then as she wiped them away with a small lace-edged handkerchief, she rose to her feet and walked towards the door.

As she reached it she turned back to say in a voice that was hoarse and broken:

"Tell your father when he comes back that if he has any compassion in his heart, or any feeling of decency, he must come to me. I have to see him—do you understand?"

"Yes, of course," Honora answered, "I will tell Papa."

Lady Studleigh had not said any more. She had gone from the Drawing-Room, and Honora had pitied her.

She knew her father was escorting a new interest in his life, and when he returned, looking exceedingly handsome and with a light in his eyes that showed he had enjoyed himself, Honora told him what had occurred.

"Noreen Studleigh had no right to come here worrying you," he said. "It is an extraordinary thing that women never seem to know when the game is over."

"Is that what it is, Papa? A game?"

"Of course that is what it is," her father had said. "A game in which two people are meant to enjoy themselves with no regrets and no recriminations."

"But Lady Studleigh was crying, Papa."

"Women can cry very easily when they cannot get their own way," her father said. "I am sorry, Honora, that you may think me hard, but there is nothing I can do about it."

"If you saw her, Papa, would it not make it better?"

"No, worse!" her father replied. "Lady Studleigh wants what I cannot give her."

Honora did not speak for a moment; then, as if she was working it out for herself, she asked:

"Is that love, Papa?"

"I suppose you could call it that," her father answered, "but love, my darling, is something that cannot be turned on like a tap. Either it is there or it is not, and no amount of tears, words, or pleas can produce it."

When she was alone, Honora thought over what he had said and was sure he was right.

'Our feelings are something which cannot be forced,' she thought, 'and love must be the same.'

She thought now as she drove in a carriage towards Grosvenor Square that it was going to be very difficult to love Aunt Aline.

"I must try to love her," she reasoned with herself, "because she and Uncle George are all I have left to remind me of Papa."

When she said good-bye to Sister Benedict, who had brought her to London, and to the other pupils who were being carried on to their homes, she felt as if she was saying good-bye to everything that was safe and familiar and embarking on an unknown sea which was rough and very unpredictable.

However, Dalton, the Butler, welcomed her as she entered the Hall.

"Nice to see you home, Miss Honora!" he said. "I hope you've had a good journey."

"Yes, thank you," Honora replied. "Is my uncle here?"

"He'll be back shortly, Miss, but Her Ladyship's waiting for you in the Drawing-Room."

He preceded Honora up the elegantly carved staircase and opened the double mahogany doors of the Drawing-Room with a flourish.

"Miss Honora, M'Lady!" he announced.

Honora saw that her aunt was sitting at the far end of the room.

There was a fire burning in the grate although it was a warm spring day, and the room was fragrant with the scent of hot-house flowers.

Her aunt, dazzlingly beautiful in a crimson silk gown, watched Honora's approach.

There was no welcome in her dark eyes, and as her niece drew nearer to her, there was a sudden tightening of her lips.

Although Honora was not aware of it, she was far more lovely than the Countess remembered or had expected.

"So you have arrived!" she said in a tone which did not sound very pleased.

Honora curtseyed.

"I am afraid I am a little late, Aunt Aline, but it has

been a long journey, and it was very rough crossing the Channel."

The Countess seemed to look her up and down before she said:

"I expect you want to change, but as I am going out, I want to talk to you before you do so. You had better sit down and listen to what I have to say."

"Yes, of course, Aunt Aline," Honora said obediently, and seated herself in a chair opposite her aunt's.

Her eyes were full of admiration as she looked at the picture her aunt made, posed for effect—for it could hardly have been an accident—in a high-backed chair covered in petit-point.

It picked out the colour of her gown, while her dark hair was silhouetted against a huge vase of Madonna lilies.

"You look, Aunt Aline, as if you ought to be hanging in the Uffizi Gallery!" Honora said impulsively, and just for an instant the hard look in Aline Langstone's eyes softened.

Then she said, glancing at the clock:

"I have to leave in five minutes, and what I have to tell you will not take long."

"What is it, Aunt Aline?"

She had the uncomfortable feeling that her aunt was going to say something momentous that concerned herself.

She wondered if she was to be sent away somewhere else rather than be allowed to stay with her uncle and aunt. And, if so, she had the idea that it might be unpleasant.

There was a little pause as if the Countess was feeling for words. Then she said in a voice that had no warmth in it:

"You are an extremely fortunate young woman! In fact, I do not know of any girl who on coming from School could hear anything as marvellous and miraculous as what I am going to tell you."

Honora looked puzzled.

She was very sensitive and perceptive, and while her aunt's words sounded almost triumphant, the tone in

which she spoke gave Honora the feeling that what she
was to learn from her aunt would be disagreeable.

She therefore did not make any answer, but only waited.
Her eyes, which unexpectedly were grey, seemed to hold
the sunshine, as did her hair, which was very fair.

Because she had been travelling for so long, little curls
had escaped from under her bonnet onto her oval forehead.

There was a hard note in Aline Langstone's voice as she
said, as if the words were jerked from between her lips:

"It may come as a surprise, but you are to be married to
the Duke of Tynemouth!"

For a moment Honora thought she could not have heard
her a-right and must have misunderstood. Her aunt surely
could not have said what she thought she had.

Then, as the Countess did not speak again, she asked in
bewilderment:

"D-did you . . . say I am to . . . marry somebody?"

"The Duke of Tynemouth, the most eligible, the most
wealthy, and the most important bachelor in the whole of
England! No young girl as unimportant as you has ever
been honoured in such a way before."

"But . . . but I do not . . . know him!"

"What has that to do with it?" her aunt asked sharply.
"He will call to see you in two hours' time, when I shall
have returned, and your engagement will be announced
tomorrow."

Honora made a helpless little gesture with her hands.

"I find it difficult to understand what you are . . . saying
to me. I had hoped . . . of course to . . . marry someday, but
I could not . . . possibly marry . . . . a man I have never . . . seen
and about whom I know . . . nothing."

"That is the sort of idiotic remark I would expect from a
girl of your age," the Countess snapped. "Try to get it into
your stupid head that the Duke is the greatest catch in the
whole country. Every parent with a marriageable daughter
has been down on their knees begging him to become
their son-in-law, and now you have been lucky enough to
be chosen as his wife."

Aline Langstone drew in her breath before she added:

"You can thank God for such a blessing. I presume at the Convent you were taught to do that when your prayers were answered?"

Honora drew in her breath.

"I hoped to marry sometime, and of course I have . . . thought about it, Aunt Aline, but I imagined it would be to . . . somebody I loved, as Mama loved Papa."

"I should have thought you were old enough by now," the Countess replied, "to realise that your father should never in any circumstances have married your mother."

"Why should you say that?"

"Because, you foolish child, your father with his looks and his family background should have married a girl with money. Your mother was very pretty, I am not denying that, but she had nothing else to recommend her!"

The Countess's voice was scornful as she went on:

"That was why, as you must have been aware, your parents lived from hand to mouth, and when your father died he owed thousands of pounds, for which your uncle made himself responsible."

"I only wish," Honora said in a low voice, "that I could have paid back that money . . . myself. I did thank Uncle George . . . at the time, and I will thank him again . . . just as I am very . . . grateful to him for paying my . . . School fees."

"You can express your gratitude in a far better way than by words, for paying him back is exactly what you will be able to do in a hundred different ways, when you are married to the Duke."

Honora was very pale and said in a voice that seemed to be strangled in her throat:

"H-how can I . . . marry him?"

"It will all be arranged," her aunt answered. "Leave everything to me, and if you have any doubts and wish to make a lot of foolish remarks about it, you are not to make them to your uncle."

Honora looked at her aunt wide-eyed, and the Countess went on:

"All you have to do is exactly what I tell you, and the

first thing is to go upstairs and take off your travelling-clothes and change into something respectable. I suppose you have a decent gown of some sort?"

She paused. Then, as if it was difficult to say the words pleasantly, she added:

"We shall be concentrating on your trousseau as soon as the engagement is annoucced, and you must certainly have something fashionable to wear before you meet anybody."

The Countess glanced at the clock again and rose to her feet.

"That is all I have to say for the moment, and I can only repeat that you are very, very fortunate. But do not try to draw a parallel between your life and your parents', for there has not been and will not be in the future any resemblance whatsoever!"

With that, like a ship at full sail, her red skirts rustling as she moved, the Countess swept across the room.

She opened the door, and the Butler must have been standing outside, for Honora heard her say:

"See that somebody shows Miss Honora to her room, Dalton, and I suppose the carriage is waiting for me?"

"Yes, M'Lady."

"I shall be back in about an hour's time. I am expecting His Grace the Duke of Tynemouth to call at six o'clock."

"Very good, M'Lady."

She must now have been walking down the stairs, but Honora did not move from where she was standing.

She felt as though she had been hit on the head, and it was hard to think.

It was almost as if the room were whirling round her, and the floor seemed as unsteady as that in the ship crossing the Channel.

"Married! How can I be . . . married?"

She felt as if she had asked the question out loud, but her lips had not moved.

Then a woman came into the Drawing-Room whose face she recognised. It was Mrs. Morton, the Housekeeper, whom she had known in the past.

"Good-afternoon, Miss Honora," Mrs. Morton said. "Nice to see you back, and how you've grown!"

"Quite a lot, I think," Honora smiled, "and I am very glad you are still here."

"Of course I'm still here," Mrs. Morton replied. "Thirty-one years I've been with His Lordship, and I like to think he'd find it hard to do without me."

"I am sure he would," Honora replied.

"Come upstairs, Miss Honora. Her Ladyship wants you changed and dressed before she returns, and the footmen have brought up your luggage."

Mrs. Morton led the way from the Drawing-Room and up the stairs which led to the next floor.

It was only later that Honora realised she was not in the small single room that she had occupied before when she had stayed with her uncle and aunt in Grosvenor Square, but in one of the best Guest-Rooms which overlooked the garden in the Square.

"You'll be comfortable here, Miss," Mrs. Morton was saying, smiling affably.

Honora's two small trunks had been unstrapped and opened by the footmen, and now two housemaids were taking out the clothes she had brought with her from Florence.

They were simple, but one of them was a very pretty day-gown which she had bought from a friend who had grown out of it, and which originally had come from an expensive dressmaker in Paris.

It was a young girl's gown of very pale blue silk, the skirt was very full and the waist tiny, and the bodice of soft material had a tiny edging of lace that was exceedingly becoming.

When Honora had it on, Mrs. Morton looked at her with admiration.

"You're as lovely as your mother, Miss, an' that's a fact! When I first sees her with your father after they was married, I thought she was the prettiest lady I'd seen in my life!"

"I thought that too," Honora said, "and if I am only a little like her I will be very proud."

"You're very like her, and that's something nobody would dispute," Mrs. Morton replied, "only your hair's a bit fairer."

"Perhaps it will darken when I grow older," Honora suggested.

Mrs. Morton laughed.

"I think that's unlikely, and most young ladies would be very pleased to have hair that looked like the sunshine or spring flowers. Let Emily arrange it for you, Miss. She's very good with hair."

Emily arranged ringlets on either side of Honora's cheeks, and when she had finished, both she and the other housemaids stared at her with admiration.

"You look like a piece of Dresden china, Miss Honora, an' that's the truth!" Emily said.

As she spoke, Honora looked at the other maid and knew they were both thinking that Her Ladyship would not be pleased.

When the two maids had carried the two empty trunks outside the room, Mrs. Morton stood behind Honora, who was sitting in front of the mirror on the dressing-table, and said:

"You look worried, Miss Honora. What's troubling you?"

"I suppose it is coming back to England and knowing that I cannot see... Papa, and I have been... away for such a long time," Honora replied.

"You mustn't feel like that, Miss," Mrs. Morton said kindly. "Her Ladyship's got big plans for you, and I'm sure you'll be a great success, looking as you do."

From the way she spoke, Honora was sure that Mrs. Morton was aware that she was to marry the Duke.

She thought that even if the servants had not been told, they would have listened at the key-holes or when they were waiting at table, and would be aware of what was to take place.

She would have felt more apprehensive than she was already if she had known that the previous evening after the Duke had left, her uncle and aunt had had what might be described as a "stand-up fight."

"You have agreed to what?" the Earl had thundered in a voice that could be heard through the closed door by the footman on duty outside.

"Do not shout at me, George!" the Countess replied. "I told you quite clearly that Ulric Tynemouth has agreed to marry Honora."

"He has never seen the girl!"

"No, but he has seen the Princess, and that is quite enough for him!"

"Are you telling me you hatched up this plot for him to marry my niece so that he will not be compelled to take Prince Albert's cousin as his wife?"

"That is exactly what I told you, George, if you had been listening," his wife answered, "and whatever Honora is like now, after being two years in Florence, at least she could not be as plain as Princess Sophie or so incredibly dull."

"In the first place, you had no right to tell Tynemouth what I told you in confidence," the Earl retorted, "and I have never heard such a ridiculous idea in my life, in which I will have no part!"

"What will you do?"

"What will I do?" the Earl repeated. "I will tell Tynemouth firmly and categorically that I will not give him my permission to marry Honora, and if he wants a decoy to avert the Queen's attention from him he can find somebody else's niece!"

The Countess laughed and it was not a very pleasant sound.

"Really, George, how can you make such a fool of yourself? You know as well as I do that any of our acquaintances would go down on their knees and lick the floor if it ensured that the Duke would be their son-in-law!"

Her voice was deliberately sad as she went on:

"Unfortunately, we have not a daughter we can offer

him, but he has agreed, actually agreed to marry Honora! You must realise what that will mean!"

There was silence before the Earl said slowly:

"I imagine from your point of view it means you will see more of Tynemouth than you do already, and that is too much!"

As if the note in her husband's voice was a warning to the Countess, she changed her tactics.

She knew only too well how to manage her husband, as she managed other men.

She gave a little laugh and moved towards him.

"George, darling, you are jealous! How adorable of you, and it makes me very happy!"

She put her arms round his neck and turned her beautiful face up to his as she said:

"Nobody knows better than you do that it amuses me to flirt with the Duke, and it is certainly a feather in my cap that he is so attentive, but no man has ever found me anything but cold and unresponsive."

She moved a little closer as she said:

"It is something you have often accused me of yourself, and you know how much I love you."

Aline was pulling his head down to hers and her body was very soft. The Earl somewhat reluctantly put his arms round her.

The exotic French perfume she used seemed somehow to dull his senses.

"It is all very well, Aline . . ." he began.

Then his wife's lips were on his and he was unable to say any more.

Only when she released him did he say:

"We have to talk about this, you know."

"There is nothing to say, dearest George," the Countess replied. "The Duke has promised to marry Honora, and because he must be a step ahead of the Queen, the engagement will be announced tomorrow. So you and I must tell everybody that it was arranged a year ago when she was too young to be married."

"I doubt if anybody will believe that."

His tone was reluctant, but the Countess knew she had won the battle, and she merely replied:

"All those women who have tried to catch him either for their daughters or for themselves will be grinding their teeth with envy. Just leave everything to me, George, and all you have to do is to buy Honora a trousseau which will cost a great deal of money, which you can well afford."

"You are going too fast, Aline," the Earl expostulated. "I have not given my consent to this ridiculous scheme, and I do not intend..."

He stopped because he realised that his wife was not listening but was in fact leaving the room.

"We must go and dress for dinner, George," she said. "Have you forgotten that we are dining with the Devonshires? Of course do not breathe a word about the engagement until Honora has actually arrived in the country."

The Earl had a great deal more to say, but as the room was empty he would have been talking to himself.

It was only when he walked slowly to his dressing-room that it suddenly struck him that once Tynemouth was married, he might not be quite the menace he suspected him of being at the moment.

* * *

Honora paused at the top of the stairs which would take her down to the Drawing-Room.

As she did so, she heard somebody come into the Hall below her.

Langstone House was built with a staircase curving up to the third floor, and the rather ugly dome which lighted it resulted in voices having a decided echo that was at times disconcerting.

But it also enabled anyone on the other floors to have a "bird's-eye view" of the Hall.

As she stood with her hand on the bannisters, she realised that the Butler was taking a hat, stick, and gloves from a man who had just entered, and, with a little restriction of her heart, she guessed he was the Duke.

Unable to move, she watched him climb the staircase

below her and saw how tall he was and how square-shouldered.

While she could not see his face clearly, she was well aware that he had not only an outstanding figure but a presence which gave him exactly the right image to portray his importance.

For the first time she realised that if she married him, as her aunt had told her she must, she would be a Duchess.

She found the idea frightening, just as she was frightened of the man who was to be her husband.

'It is impossible . . . it is something I . . . cannot do,' she thought unhappily.

She felt as if her aunt had numbed her mind by the hard blows of what she had told her, and it was impossible to think or begin to calculate how she could prevent herself from being married to a stranger in such an unseemly manner.

"Mama would have been shocked, and Papa would, I am quite certain, have violently opposed it," she told herself.

Then she was not quite certain.

After all, her father had always liked being invited to important houses by their distinguished owners.

At times he had laughed about the invitations he received.

"I am off to the Duke of Marlborough's on Wednesday," he had told Honora a month before he was killed, "which means I shall ride the best horses, drink the best wine, and enjoy myself in the company of the most distinguished people in England. What do you think of that?"

"It sounds thrilling, Papa!"

There was just a hint of mischief in Honora's eyes before she asked:

"Why did they ask you?"

"I will tell you exactly why," he said. "It is because I am extremely good company. I amuse people and make them laugh, and while the men think I am a good sportsman, the women . . ."

He paused and added:

"Never mind about the women!"

"But you are not rich and important like all the people with whom you spend so much time," Honora remarked.

"I know that, and that is why it is so gratifying," her father answered. "You will find, my darling, when you are grown up, that the rich are often bored with themselves, and most of them need a Court Jester or somebody who is sympathetic to their troubles. You may not believe it, but they have them!"

Then he was laughing, and Honora cried:

"Dukes, Princes, or Marquises, I do not believe that anybody, Papa, could be as attractive or as much fun as you are!"

"That is exactly what I am, and what I want them to think," her father said, smiling.

He had gone off to Blenheim Palace and returned to find a dozen more invitations to other important houses where he could enjoy himself. It made Honora long for the day when she would be old enough to accompany him.

At the same time, she thought now that while her father might have been impressed by the Duke, he would certainly not want her to marry a man with whom she was not in love and who obviously was not in love with her.

"Why does he want to marry me?" she asked herself.

She had no answer, but she was quite sure that there must be a reason, and that it was not a straight-forward or particularly pleasant one.

Because she knew it was expected of her, she went down to the Drawing-Room.

As Dalton opened the double doors for her, she had a feeling that she was stepping into a Play of which she did not know the plot, nor even whether it would be a romance or a tragedy.

As she entered the room, her aunt was standing at the far end of it in front of the fireplace, looking up at the Duke, who was standing beside her.

They not only appeared extremely attractive, but Honora thought it was obvious that they were very close and personal friends.

She was not certain how she knew this, it was just as if it

vibrated on the atmosphere towards her, and she did not question the truth of it.

She was halfway down the room before first the Duke was aware of her and turned his head in her direction. Then her aunt did the same.

"Oh, there you are, Honora!" she exclaimed.

As she spoke, her eyes flickered over her niece's appearance and there was a hard look in them.

Then as Honora drew nearer still, the Countess managed to say in a voice which sounded almost as if she forced the words from between her lips:

"Let me introduce to you, dear child, the Duke of Tynemouth! Ulric, this is Honora!"

Because she felt shy, Honora found it very hard to look at him, but because she knew it was bad manners not to do so, she raised her grey eyes to his face as she made a respectful curtsey.

The Duke bowed, and as he looked at her she had the uncomfortable feeling not only that he was taking in her appearance but that it was almost as if he expected to find something he disliked.

It was not what she had expected to feel about him, and almost as if it were a warning signal, she told herself that just as she had no wish to marry him, the Duke had no wish to marry her.

Then why? Why? Why?

The question seemed almost as if it were floating in the air round her, whispered in the crackle of the fire, and even carried on the fragrance of the flowers.

"I am delighted to meet you, Miss Lang!" the Duke said in a deep voice.

As he spoke, Honora knew that he was not delighted.

In which case, why, why, had he asked to marry her?

Chapter Three

They had a stilted conversation for a few minutes, the Duke asking in a rather bored voice what Honora's journey had been like from France, and the Countess answering before she could say it had been rough in the Channel.

Then, in a somewhat exaggerated and theatrical voice and with an expression in her dark eyes that Honora did not like to interpret, her aunt said:

"I am going to leave you together for a few minutes, but I will not be long."

She looked at the Duke in a meaningful manner, then moved towards the door, very conscious as she did so of her graceful carriage and the rustle of her full skirts over the carpet.

As she reached the door she looked back and again she was looking at the Duke and not at Honora.

The door closed behind her, and there was an uncomfortable silence until the Duke said:

"I think your aunt will have told you that we are to be married."

Honora drew in her breath. Then she said:

"That is what Aunt Aline told me, but I cannot understand, Your Grace, why you should wish to marry me when we have never met until this moment."

She thought the Duke looked surprised.

Then, feeling embarrassed, she stared down into the fire, aware that she was trembling because she was frightened.

After what seemed a very long pause the Duke said:

"I think you must be aware that marriages in families like mine and your uncle's are usually arranged."

As he spoke, Honora was distinctly aware that he was feeling for words and that what he had said was not the real reason for their marriage.

"I should have . . . thought," she said hesitatingly, "that . . . even so . . . it was usual for the prospective . . . bride and bridegroom to . . . meet before anything was . . . decided."

The Duke made an impatient gesture with his hand, and then as if making up his mind he said:

"I think if we are to be married it would be wise for us to be frank with each other."

Honora looked up at him as she replied:

"That is what I would . . . like, and I would therefore be . . . grateful . . . Your Grace . . . if you would tell me the . . . real reason why the announcement should appear in the newspapers . . . tomorrow morning."

"Your aunt has not told you?"

"No; all she said when I arrived an hour or so ago was that we were to be married."

"Very well, I will tell you the truth," the Duke said. "I expected to have an arranged marriage sooner or later, but there seemed to be no particular hurry."

Honora was listening intently, her eyes on his face as he went on:

"I learnt, and it was actually your aunt who informed me of it, that Her Majesty the Queen wishes me to marry Prince Albert's niece, Princess Sophie of Saxe-Coburg-Gotha."

The Duke's voice was hard and almost aggressive as he spoke, and after a little pause Honora said:

"And that is . . . something you do not . . . wish to do?"

"Certainly not!" the Duke replied sharply. "I have met the Princess, and I can assure you she is the last woman I would in any circumstances willingly take as my wife!"

"And yet you are . . . prepared to . . . ask me! Why?"

Honora saw that her question had, for the moment, surprised him. Then as if he sought for an answer he said:

"You are English, and you belong to a family for whom I have a great respect."

"But . . . surely," Honora persisted, "there must be many . . . other families who come into the same category, and you . . . therefore have a wide choice. So why me?"

The Duke put out his hand and, as if he needed support, held on to the mantelpiece. Then looking down at the fire he answered:

"I understood from your aunt that the marriage would meet with your approval, and . . ."

He paused, and there was silence before Honora asked: "What is the other reason?"

"Quite frankly, I have to act quickly. I suspect that when I am on duty at Buckingham Palace tomorrow, Her Majesty will suggest that the Princess would make me a suitable wife."

Again there was that harsh note in the Duke's voice which revealed his feelings very clearly.

"So I suppose I am the lesser of two evils!" Honora remarked.

The Duke looked at her as if in surprise that she should speak in such a way before he said:

"I have a feeling, Miss Lang, that this conversation should not be taking place, and we are perhaps making things very much more difficult than they are already."

"The only difficulty, Your Grace, is that you have no wish to marry me, and I have no wish to marry anybody I do not . . . love."

If she had dropped a bomb at his feet the Duke could not have been more surprised.

He was so used to being pursued, enticed, and implored to marry that he had never really considered that any unmarried girl to whom he proposed would hesitate before accepting him.

Now it was as if he was seeing her for the first time, and he asked:

"Are you saying categorically, Miss Lang, that you will not accept me as your husband?"

"I am afraid it will make Aunt Aline very . . . angry,"

Honora replied, "but knowing what your . . . true feelings are in the matter, and that I am only a convenient means of escape from . . . something you have no wish to do . . . my answer is therefore quite simply 'no'!"

As if there was nothing more to say, she turned and walked towards the door. At that moment it opened and the Countess came back into the room.

As she did so, she was aware that she had not left the Duke and Honora together for long.

Because the girl was looking so unexpectedly lovely and very elegant in a manner she had not expected, Aline Langstone was driven by an irrepressible jealousy to prevent her from being any longer alone with the Duke.

Then as she came into the room and saw the expression of consternation on the Duke's face while Honora walked towards the door, she asked sharply: "What is happening? Where are you going?"

Honore stopped and stood still, and the Duke replied: "Miss Lang has refused me!"

There was a note of surprise in his voice, and yet at the same time it was as if he challenged Aline and told her that as he had thought at first, her idea would not work.

"Refused you?" the Countess exclaimed, her voice rising shrilly.

"I am . . . sorry if it annoys you, Aunt Aline," Honora said, "but . . . His Grace has been frank with me and told me the reason for such a . . . precipitate engagement . . . and I am sure he will be able to find . . . somebody far more . . . suitable to . . . marry him than I am."

She tried to speak calmly and with dignity, but she could not prevent a little tremor on her words that showed she was afraid.

Her aunt looked at her and Honora was aware of a fury in her eyes before she said:

"Come with me, Honora, I wish to speak to you alone."

Then as she turned she said over her shoulder:

"Help yourself to a drink, Ulric. There is a bottle of champagne in the ice-cooler."

She did not wait for his reply but stalked ahead of

Honora to the door, and there was nothing she could do but follow her.

Outside, her aunt moved down the passage that led towards her bedroom and entered her *Boudoir*, which was actually only two doors away from the Drawing-Room.

Honora followed her inside, aware once again of the fragrance of carnations and lilies mingling with the French perfume that her aunt always used.

As she shut the door behind them the Countess was standing in the centre of the room, and her face was contorted with a terrifying expression of venom and anger.

"May I ask you," she said, "what you think you are playing at?"

"P-please . . . Aunt Aline," Honora replied, "try to understand . . . the Duke has no wish to marry me, nor I him!"

"Do you really think, you little fool," the Countess demanded, "that you can upset my plans and do anything but obey me?"

"You cannot . . . force me into a . . . marriage that could not be anything but . . . unhappy!"

"If your poverty-stricken father were alive," the Countess replied, "he would be overwhelmed with delight that you should marry anybody so important and so rich! It would mean that he would be able to sponge on his son-in-law instead of on every other Tom, Dick, and Harry from whom he could borrow money."

"That is . . . not true!" Honora cried.

At the same time, she had the uncomfortable feeling that there was a grain of truth in it and that her father would have been delighted for her to marry the Duke of Tynemouth.

"And how do you think," the Countess continued, "that you, without a penny to your name and nothing to recommend you except that you are a Lang, are going to find another husband half as suitable as the Duke?"

"Whoever he may be," Honora replied, "perhaps I would be . . . in love with him."

"Love!" the Countess said contemptuously. "If that is

the rubbish with which they have stuffed your head at the Convent, then all I can say is that your uncle's money has been wasted!"

Honora did not answer, and the Countess's eyes narrowed as she said:

"As you are obviously too half-witted to think for yourself, I intend to think for you and give you a choice."

"A . . . choice?"

"Yes, a choice," her aunt replied. "It is quite simple—either you marry the Duke as I have planned, or you go into a Convent and become a Nun!"

Honora stared at her in sheer amazement as she went on:

"It would not be a nice, comfortable, rich Convent such as you have just left! One of the Charities to which your uncle most generously subscribes is known as the 'Little Sisters of the Poor,' who devote themselves to caring for the sick and poverty-stricken in the slums or wearing out their knees in prayer."

She paused, and her face was very spiteful as she went on:

"I also understand that they give up everything they possess, and that should certainly be easy for you, since you possess nothing anyway!"

"Are you . . . really suggesting," Honora faltered, "that I should take the . . . v-veil?"

"That is what you will have to do," her aunt replied, "unless of course you are prepared to starve in the gutter."

"You . . . cannot mean it," Honora said. "Please . . . could I have more time to . . . consider what I should . . . do?"

"There is no time," the Countess snapped. "You must make up your mind here and now to marry the Duke, or I will arrange for you to be taken tomorrow morning to the Convent."

She gave a laugh which was an unpleasant one before she added:

"You must be aware that a Guardian has complete and absolute control over his Ward, and if your uncle sends you to a Convent, there is no appeal against his decision."

She looked at Honora as she spoke, saw that her face was very white and she was trembling, and added spitefully:

"The choice is yours. There is no other alternative, and however mentally half-witted you may be, I should have thought it would not be difficult for you to make up your mind."

Honora was defeated and she knew it.

"I . . . I have no . . . vocation to be a . . . Nun," she said in a very small voice, "and . . . therefore . . . if you insist . . . I will . . . m-marry the Duke."

"Good!" her aunt said quickly. "I will go explain to him that you were just overcome by the importance of his position and that was why you refused him. In the meantime, get out of my sight! Go up to your bedroom and stay there! Even to look at you makes me feel sick!"

As she spoke, the Countess opened the door of her *Boudoir* and hurried back along the passage to the Drawing-Room.

Honora stood for several minutes without moving.

Then she put her hands up to her face and covered her eyes. She asked herself how this could possibly have happened, but she knew now there was nothing she could do about it.

* * *

The Countess entered the Drawing-Room, shut the door quietly behind her, and moved swiftly towards the Duke, who was still standing beside the fireplace.

As she reached him he looked at her to say:

"This is a nice mess!"

"It is nothing of the sort, darling," she said. "The girl was just overcome by you and the whole situation, and who shall blame her? Now she has agreed to do exactly what we want, and the footman can take the notice of the engagement to the newspapers."

"What you mean," the Duke said slowly, "is that you have bullied her into saying she will marry me."

"She is just frightened and bewildered at the idea of becoming a Duchess," Aline replied. "Oh, my dearest man, if only I were in her shoes!"

The Duke smiled and it swept away the frown between his eyes.

"I am not certain," he said in a very different voice, "that you would make a very good Duchess."

"The only thing that could matter," Aline said passionately, "would be that I was your wife."

She lifted her face to his as she spoke, and as if he could not help himself the Duke put his arms round her and kissed her lips.

Then, fearing they might be disturbed, he released her to ask:

"Are you quite certain there is nothing else we can do? I did not expect your niece to refuse me."

"But you told her the reason why you were doing it."

"She asked me to tell her the truth, and it seemed better for me to tell her than that she should hear it sooner or later from somebody else."

Aline shrugged her shoulders as she said:

"I think that was rather foolish of you. After all, young girls are always excessively romantic and have their heads in the clouds. It would have been far better if you had just let her think you were a Knight on a white charger."

"I could hardly expect the girl, having never seen me before, not to ask questions."

"If you had asked me to marry you," Aline said, "I would have asked only one question, and that would be—'when?'"

The way she spoke as she moved nearer to him, her eyes seeming to sparkle with the fire burning within her, made the Duke draw in his breath.

There was something about Aline Langstone that aroused his desire as few other women had been able to do.

And yet at the back of his mind some cynical voice told him that it was a very physical emotion, and one he would not find particularly desirable in his wife.

What was more, if he was honest, he knew that the way Aline behaved and even the strength of her feelings for him were things he would find very reprehensible in a young girl.

"I am not talking of you, Aline, but of your niece," he said, "and I am upset by her attitude."

"Leave Honora to me," Aline Langstone said. "All girls are the same and take up the contrary view to anything which is suggested to them."

She knew the Duke was still worried and added:

"As a matter of fact, when she was alone with me she said that she thought you were extremely attractive and would like to marry you if you really wanted her to."

"Are you sure she said that?" the Duke asked.

Aline laughed.

"Do you really believe there exists a woman who is not bowled over by you as soon as she sees you, and would not give her right hand for the honour and privilege of being your wife?"

She spoke very convincingly; then, as if to make sure the Duke was certain that he was doing the right thing, she added:

"Darling, be sensible. I know this has been somewhat of a rush, but surely anything is better than having to look at Princess Sophie for the rest of your life."

The Duke gave a shudder and said:

"That, of course, is indisputable!"

"I think you have forgotten," Aline went on in a low voice, "how easy and wonderful it will be for us to be able to see so much more of each other than we can now."

The idea excited her and she continued:

"We will go to the Dawlishes this weekend as we promised, then the following week I think we should all stay with you at Tyne Castle."

"I think actually," the Duke said, as if he was thinking it over, "it would be best to give up the Dawlishes. As soon as the engagement is announced tomorrow, all my family will want to meet my future bride, and to save ourselves a whole succession of boring luncheons and dinners, let us get it over all at once by inviting them to the Castle this weekend."

Aline clapped her hands.

"Of course, you are right! You are always right, and it will be perfect for us to be at the Castle together!"

She paused before she said:

"Besides, now that I think of it, the following weekend George and I ought to give a party at home and plan the wedding."

"The wedding?" the Duke asked suspiciously.

"There is no point in having a long engagement," Aline said, "and the sooner we have a respectable excuse for being together at the Castle regularly, the sooner will George realise there is no reasonable way in which we can go on refusing your invitations."

"Actually," the Duke said, "I was surprised that he agreed to such a precipitate engagement."

Aline smiled.

"He did make a slight protest last night, and he was very angry with me for having told you about Princess Sophie. But I told him that it was a marvellous opportunity for Honora to make a good marriage."

She laughed and added:

"I also convinced him, with great cleverness, that I was to you what he had always found and accused me of being: a very cold woman!"

Laughing softly, she lifted her lips to the Duke to say in a low, passionate voice that seemed to vibrate on the air between them:

"Do you find me cold, Ulric?"

His arms went round her before she had finished speaking, and he kissed her until they were both burning with a fiery desire that made it impossible to think of anything else. . . .

* * *

The following morning, as Honora was called, Emily put two newspapers down on the bed in front of her.

"It's in the Court Column, Miss," she said, "an' it reads ever so exciting. I knew you'd want to see it, so I brings up the newspapers before 'is Lordship goes down to breakfast."

There was no need for Honora to ask what she was

talking about, for the previous night when she had dined alone with her uncle and aunt, they had both talked of nothing but her engagement.

"I think you should have let me see the announcement before you sent it to *The Gazette* and the other newspapers," the Earl was saying sharply as she entered the Drawing-Room before dinner.

"I am sorry, dearest, but I did not think you would be interested," Aline replied, "and I really wrote it out quite correctly."

"I hope so."

Then as the Earl saw Honora advancing towards them, he smiled and held out his hands, saying:

"How are you, my dear? I am delighted to see you after such a long absence."

Because of the warmth in his voice and the definite resemblance she could see in him to her father, Honora ran towards him.

"It is lovely to see you, Uncle George!" she exclaimed, and kissed his cheek.

"Well, well!" the Earl said, looking at her. "You have certainly grown into a pretty young lady! Your father, if he were alive, would be very proud of you!"

"I hope so, Uncle George, because as you know, Papa always disliked plain women."

Her uncle laughed.

"That is certainly true, and I have always thought that my brother and I managed to marry the two most beautiful and charming women in the world!"

It flashed through Honora's mind that while that was true where her mother was concerned, her aunt might be beautiful but she was certainly not charming.

In fact, she knew if she was truthful that she greatly disliked her.

"I hope, George," the Countess interrupted, "that pretty speech means that you will be very generous over Honora's trousseau."

Honora knew as her aunt spoke that she was pointing out to her once again how grateful she had to be to her

uncle for providing for her as her father had lamentably
failed to do.

"I . . . I will try not to be too . . . extravagant, Uncle
George," she said.

"Of course you must be dressed as befits your future
position as the Duchess of Tynemouth," her uncle replied.

There was something in the way he spoke the name that
told Honora, although she had no reason for thinking it,
that her uncle did not like the Duke.

Then she told herself she must be mistaken because
obviously the Duke was a close friend of both her uncle
and her aunt.

"Now you are not to make Honora feel shy," Aline
interrupted, as if she was afraid of what she might say,
"and frighten her when she realises how much is to be
done before we can stay at the Castle next weekend."

"Is that what we are doing?" the Earl asked.

"It may seem a bore to you, darling," the Countess
answered, "but obviously the Duke's relations, and there
are far too many of them, will want to meet his future
bride, and as he said himself, it would be better to get it
over and done with all at once.

""There is certainly something in that," the Earl agreed,
"and I hope you are not going to let me in for a whole lot
of dinner-parties. You know I dislike them, and what is
more, I have to be at the Palace most of next week."

"I will save you from as much as I can," his wife said
caressingly, "but I am sure Honora will want your support,
and you will be so much better than I would be at advising
her about what she should and should not do."

As she spoke, Aline was thinking that the more respon-
sibility she could make her husband assume, the more
time she would have to be alone with the Duke.

With a smile that seemed almost natural she said now to
her niece:

"I feel sure, Honora, you will want to feel that you can
depend on your uncle and turn to him with all your
problems."

"I do not . . . want to be a . . . nuisance."

"You will not be that, my dear," the Earl assured her genially, "and I know too how much you must miss your father. I miss him too. Everything always seemed so much more amusing when he was there."

"He was always . . . laughing," Honora said in a low voice. "I think it is his laughter I miss more than . . . anything else."

The Butler announced dinner, and when they were seated in the large, rather pompous Dining-Room, the Countess went out of her way to indicate to the Earl how much Honora needed his help.

She also kept asserting how important it was that Honora, being so young and inexperienced, should not make any mistakes.

"You know as well as I do, George," she said, "how all those spiteful women who have tried to marry Ulric off to their unattractive daughters will be waiting to find fault with poor little Honora."

"I am quite certain they will find that a difficult thing to do," the Earl said with unexpected gallantry.

"Only if you look after her, and teach her so that she does not make *faux pas* by saying the wrong thing," the Countess said.

She paused before she added:

"It will give me great pleasure to see their faces when I dress Honora with the good taste which most of them lack, and in gowns that a great many of them cannot afford to buy."

Her aunt spoke so spitefully that Honora wondered what the ladies to whom she was referring had done to upset her. She was not aware, of course, that she hated them because they had pursued the Duke.

It struck the Countess even as she was speaking that it would be agonising to make Honora look even lovelier than she did at the moment in gowns that only the most expensive and renowned dressmakers in Bond Street could provide.

At the same time, she was aware that if she tried to make her look dowdy, which in any case would be difficult, her enemies would be sharp enough to suspect that she had a reason for it.

Although she and the Duke had been as circumspect as possible, she was not so foolish as to think that the feelings they had for each other had passed unnoticed amongst their so-called friends who watched with hawk-like eyes everything they did.

The Duke was a constant source of pleasure to them because his many love-affairs gave them a great deal to chatter about.

What they did not know, they invented, and Aline was aware that they had hated her from the first moment she swept into the Social World to take it by storm.

She came from a family whose origins were impeccable, but which, like many others, had grown poorer with each generation.

Because Aline was outstandingly beautiful, her parents had hoped she would make a good marriage.

They had therefore made tremendous sacrifices so that they could take her to London for the Season and she could make her curtsey to King William IV and Queen Adelaide.

There was no doubt that from the moment she had appeared in the Ball-Room at Buckingham Palace, positively outshining the other débutantes and drawing the eyes of every man in the room, she had been a sensation.

The invitations had poured into the house which her parents had managed to rent cheaply for three months, and from which she had been married, as if to a fanfare of trumpets.

It had been, Aline had thought later, astoundingly good luck that the Earl of Langstone had been on duty as Lord Steward on the night of her presentation and was actually standing behind the King when she made her curtsey.

William IV was famous for the remarks he made in what he thought was a *sotto voce* aside but which were usually very audible.

As Aline had swept gracefully down in front of him, he had said in what was meant to be beneath his breath:

"A pretty girl—very pretty!"

The Earl had replied somewhat pompously:

"Your Majesty's taste is always impeccable."

Aline had heard what they said, and as she rose she had given a flashing smile which had illuminated her face and had captured the heart of the Earl of Langstone.

He was acquainted with her father, and there was great excitement when an invitation arrived the following day asking them all to dinner at Langstone House in Grosvenor Square.

Aline knew, as her mother accepted, that this was the chance for which she had been waiting.

In three weeks the Earl had proposed and she had accepted him. From that moment, her future was golden in a way that she had never dared to hope it might be.

Aline had actually been shrewd, calculating, and supremely confident of her own attractions from the time she was fifteen.

She had discovered then that men of every age were attracted to her, and when she smiled at her father's contemporaries there was a "swimmy" look in their eyes as they would humbly suggest that they should kiss her in a "fatherly fashion."

She soon learnt that the word "fatherly" meant something quite different from the way her own father interpreted it.

But it gave her confidence in herself, and she was the most sophisticated and confident débutante who ever wore the Prince of Wales's three feathers on her shining head.

The Earl was besotted with her, and everything she did, from making him the most envied man at Court to making him the father of two sons, made him more and more proud.

He was at the same time extremely jealous.

But as Aline showed in their intimate moments together none of the fiery passion he had known with his mistresses before marriage, he decided that, as was only proper and to be expected of a lady, she had a cold temperament.

He had thought before the Duke appeared that one or two of his wife's admirers were becoming too intimate, and he had even considered challenging one of them to a duel.

But Aline had only laughed at him.

"How can you imagine, dearest," she had asked, "that I would look at anybody except you, and really Lord Trevor is a bore because he will not leave me alone."

She put her arms round her husband's neck as she went on:

"At the same time, he makes me feel sure that I can still attract you and you will not leave me for one of those very alluring 'love-birds' on whom you used to spend so much of your money before you knew me."

"How do you know about them?" the Earl asked sharply.

Aline laughed.

"You may be quite certain there are plenty of spiteful women to tell me exactly how you used to behave! So, dearest, I am always afraid that I shall bore you, and that once again you will make surreptitious visits to Chelsea or St. John's Wood, as you did in the past."

For a moment the Earl looked guilty. Then he said:

"I have never even seen another woman's face since I married you."

"That is what I want to believe," Aline answered, "but sometimes, because you are so attractive and of course so rich, I am afraid of losing you."

The Earl was so delighted by what she was saying to him that he forgot the conversation had started by rebuking his wife for her behaviour with Lord Trevor.

Aline could always handle him, as she was well aware, and it had been easy before the Duke had come into her life.

Then it became more difficult to conceal her indifference to the Earl's kisses and her anger when he kept repeating that she was seeing "too much of Tynemouth."

She wanted the Duke as she had never wanted any other man.

Now, she thought, the Earl would no longer have grounds for suspicion when the Duke was always in the same house-parties as they were or to resent that invariably she was seated next to him at dinner and found it difficult to talk to anybody else when he was in the room.

She thought too with satisfaction that however pretty— as she had to admit—Honora might be, she was obviously too young and too innocent to hold any interest for the Duke.

No-one knew better than Aline did that what made Ulric laugh was the witty "cut and thrust" of a conversation where every other word was an innuendo.

She was also quite certain that no other woman could evoke the same fiery response or give him the same satisfaction that she could.

'He is mine,' she thought to herself, and aloud she said: "I will take Honora shopping all tomorrow, then in the evening I will arrange a dinner-party. You must help me, George dear, by telling me which of your relations we should ask!"

The Earl groaned as she continued:

"I suppose we can be thirty, but no more. And for goodness' sake let us have some young men to offset the boredom of too many aunts and middle-aged cousins!"

This started an interchange between husband and wife of names which meant nothing to Honora, although she noticed that the majority were of people of title.

She wondered what the Duke was thinking at this moment and if, although he had no wish to marry her, he was still thinking that she was the lesser of two evils.

She felt frightened when she thought of him, and she knew that her aunt had not been speaking idly when she threatened that if she did not do as she wished, she would have to enter a Convent.

Having lived for two years in the Convent in Florence, Honora was aware that that one was very different from

the Convents where Nuns dedicated themselves either to
a life of confinement or to tending the sick and the poor.

In Florence the School was kept apart from the building
where the Nuns slept, and some of them played no part in
teaching and had no contact with the pupils.

Instead, Honora had learnt, they were segregated from
everything that appertained to the world outside.

Because some of the windows of the School looked over
the garden where these Nuns took their exercise, she
often wondered as she saw them what they thought about
and if they ever regretted having taken the veil.

She had thought, although perhaps she was wrong to do
so, that it was a waste of life as God had meant it to be
lived, and when she was very young she had once discussed
it with her mother.

"Why do some women become Nuns, Mama?" she had
asked.

The question had arisen because they had been stopped
on the road by two Nuns collecting for Charity.

"I am sure they are very good and very holy," her
mother answered, "but I cannot help feeling sorry for
them."

"Why?"

"I think God meant us, as it says in the Bible, to use our
talents and not hide them away," her mother replied.

She saw that Honora was listening and went on:

"Christ lived the life of an ordinary man, helping Joseph
with his carpentry, until He began to teach the Message
which came from God, His Father. I believe that we too
have to lead an ordinary life to the best of our abilities,
trying to do good by deeds and not entirely by prayer."

"It must be very lonely for them, Mama," Honora said.

"Perhaps I am explaining it badly," her mother went on.
"I do admire the Nuns, and of course prayer is of great
importance not only to them but to all of us, but I would
want you, my dearest, to live your life to the full."

She gave a little laugh before she added:

"And nobody does that better than your father!"

Looking back, Honora thought it was true that her

father had lived every moment of his life fully and completely and to him satisfyingly.

It had been tiresome that he had not enough money, but he enjoyed everything he did.

She had never known him not to be ready to help anyone less fortunate than himself, even though it often entailed sacrifices on the part of herself and her mother.

'No,' she thought, 'neither Papa nor Mama would wish me to go into a Convent. Therefore, as there is nothing else I can do except marry the Duke, I must try to make him . . . happy.'

She felt that this might be difficult, and she wondered what it would be like being the wife of a man who not only disliked the idea of having to marry at all but might dislike her personally.

'It is going to be very . . . very difficult,' she thought when she went to bed.

When she said her prayers she prayed fervently that both her mother and her father would help her.

"I am frightened," she told them. "Please . . . please be near me, and guide me in what I should say and do . . . and help me not to make the Duke . . . angry as Aunt Aline is angry with me."

She had the feeling that she might hear an answer to her prayer, but there was only the darkness, and as she got into bed she felt very young, inexperienced, and alone.

"Please . . . Papa and Mama . . . listen," she whispered.

But again there was no answer, only silence.

Chapter Four

*H*onora had never thought that buying clothes could be so tiring.

The next morning she had received a message to say that Her Ladyship would be waiting for her in an hour's time, and from the moment she went downstairs she felt she was running in an endless race.

First the Countess rushed her to the best and most expensive dressmaker in Bond Street and chose a dozen gowns from sketches and materials that were to be made up in record time.

She then found two gowns that were already half-finished for another customer, and by browbeating and bribery she had them diverted to Honora.

All the time she was doing this she was impressing upon Honora how fortunate she was and how she should be overwhelmed with gratitude for being treated in such an exceptional manner.

But the way her aunt spoke of her becoming a Duchess, and the almost offensively condescending manner in which she spoke to the dressmaker and her assistants, made Honora feel very uncomfortable.

She had never known her mother to be anything but sweet, kind, and polite to those who served her.

But she had already gathered that when the Countess was with her guests and people she respected, she was an entirely different person from what she was at other times.

'I hope I never become like that,' Honora thought.

She was certain that if she behaved as her mother would

wish her to do, whether she was a Duchess or her insignificant self, she would always respect other people's feelings and be pleasant to them.

However, because the dressmaker in fact was extremely impressed with all that the Countess had told her, she managed later the same afternoon to fit Honora with several gowns.

She also provided her with some exquisite nightgowns and chemises which were more beautiful than anything Honora could have imagined.

When she said so to the Countess, her aunt replied in an extremely disagreeable voice:

"The housemaids at Tyne Castle will hardly expect *my* niece to wear the rags you wore at School."

Then she added in an even more vitriolic tone:

"You could certainly not be married in them!"

The thought of this obviously put her in such a bad temper that afterwards Honora was afraid to say anything.

At the same time, she could not help being thrilled with the lovely materials and sketches which were brought for her aunt's approval, and also with the gowns that were altered for her.

She remembered how her mother had to skrimp and save to buy herself even one new dress.

She had made her own nightgowns, sewn with tiny stitches which she had learnt how to do when she was a girl, and which were the same, Honora found, as those which the Nuns used at the Convent.

Because she had felt embarrassed at spending too much of her uncle's money, she had been very economical with her clothes while she was in Florence.

She knew that for all the pupils, huge bills for books and anything appertaining to the lessons were added on to the regular fees, which were in themselves very large.

Now, because her aunt was so contemptuous of what she was wearing, she thought that perhaps she had been needlessly sensitive about it.

She would have been wiser to buy what she wanted, as

some of the other girls did, and let the Mother Superior send the bills to her uccle.

But it was too late now to think about that, and she told herself that she must be very grateful for what she was receiving.

She was not consulted as to what was purchased, but she was aware that her aunt, because she was so well dressed herself, had very good taste, and her gowns were in the very latest style and many of them came from Paris.

There were also bonnets, shawls, slippers, gloves, mittens, and a dozen more things which her aunt said she required.

All of these, after they had seen them in the shops, were brought back to the house later to be tried on in different colours and different designs.

Because everything she did seemed to annoy the Countess, it was a relief when Honora learnt, after they had returned to Grosvenor Square for luncheon, that her aunt had an appointment for the afternoon.

"Mrs. Morton will look after you," the Countess said. "I shall be returning after tea, and by that time you should have finished."

"If it is any trouble, I will not bother Mrs. Morton," Honora replied.

That was of course the wrong thing to say.

"Mrs. Morton is paid to do what I want!" the Countess snapped. "And it is correct, although you may not know it, for you to have somebody with you when tradespeople are calling."

As Honora gave a little sigh, her aunt swept away, looking as beautiful as ever, but her anger seemed to linger on the air long after she had gone.

By the time the dinner-party was about to begin, Honora thought she was almost too tired to enjoy it, and she was also feeling nervous at seeing the Duke again.

By what seemed almost a miracle, the gown that her aunt wanted her to wear arrived just half-an-hour before the guests were due to arrive, and it was without doubt the most beautiful gown Honora had ever thought of owning.

It was white, but not the rather dull, unimaginative white of a young girl's dress.

Instead, because she was to be married, it was embroidered all over with tiny silver leaves, and the bertha had the same design in silver and pearls.

When she was dressed, Honora stared at herself in the mirror, feeling that she looked like a Princess in a fairytale.

Then, as if a shadow were cast over her reflection, she remembered that where she was concerned the Prince Charming had no wish to marry her!

He was in fact resenting it, and she knew that even if he was not beside her she would feel it instinctively all through the evening.

This proved to be true, for while the Duke was being outwardly very pleasant to her relations, she could feel vibrations coming from him which told her exactly what he was really feeling.

She had always been aware that everybody had vibrations which they sent out like little rays, and ever since she had been a child she had known what other people were feeling and sometimes what they were thinking.

"Why does Papa dislike that lady who came to luncheon today?" she had asked once when she was quite small.

Her mother had looked at her in consternation.

"Did Papa tell you that?" she enquired.

Honora shook her head.

"No, but I could feel him hating her as we sat at the table, although I do not think she knew."

"I am sure she did not!" her mother exclaimed. "I think, dearest, you are mistaken."

But she had known that Honora was right, and afterwards she said to her husband:

"We must be careful what we say and do in front of Honora. The child has an almost uncanny perception in knowing what we are feeling."

Harry Lang had laughed.

"She will find that a very useful gift when she grows older," he had said, "but I am not allowing you any guesses, my darling, as to what I feel about you."

He had kissed her mother and she had forgotten about Honora for the moment, but as her daughter grew older she sometimes consulted her.

"That Governess who came to see us today and is to teach you French—did you like her, dearest?" she had enquired on one occasion.

Honora shook her head.

"No, Mama, and she was lying when she said she could speak French like a native."

"How could you know that?" her mother enquired.

"I could feel that she was lying."

Because Honora had been so positive, Mrs. Lang had chosen another teacher, and later she learnt she had been right to do so.

Although she tried not to, Honora could not help watching the Duke when he received congratulations and good wishes on their engagement.

He rather astutely managed to avoid the questions of how they had met and how long they had known each other, which almost everybody who came into the Drawing-Room was bursting with curiosity to ask.

The Countess was charming, witty, and very gracious.

Watching her, too, Honora thought it would be impossible for anybody whom she was now entertaining to realise how disagreeable she had been all day.

The difference in her voice when she spoke to them and to the Duke was very noticeable, and Honora had the frightening idea that perhaps everybody in the Social World was the same.

She had a sudden fear that she might be spending the rest of her life with people who, like her aunt, had two sides to their nature.

'I could not bear it!' she thought.

She found herself looking searchingly at all her relatives, wondering if each one of them was two-faced, and although they were gushing at her now, she thought they might easily behave very differently should the occasion arise.

It was certainly true that they were making themselves overwhelmingly pleasant, but the only time she felt less apprehensive was when an elderly great-aunt said to her quietly:

"I know that your father and mother, my dear, would both be very pleased that you are marrying somebody so distinguished. But what is more important is that Ulric, whom I have known since he was born, is very intelligent and very considerate of those who work for him on his Estates."

Honora looked at her enquiringly, and the old lady explained:

"I live only about ten miles from Tyne Castle, and as you can imagine, everybody in my village talks about the handsome Duke and has been wondering for years whom he would marry."

She gave a little chuckle as she added:

"I expect I shall have quite a lot of reflected glory because you are my great-niece."

Honora liked her and said impulsively:

"I hope, Great-Aunt Louise, that when I am living at the Castle I may come to visit you."

Her great-aunt put her hand over hers and said:

"I am always there, should you want me. Your father was my favourite nephew. He may have been naughty in many ways, but he made everybody who knew him laugh, and I miss him, as I am sure you do."

"Nothing has been the same ever since Papa... died," Honora replied.

"I heard you had been sent to Florence," her great-aunt said. "But never mind, with Ulric to look after you, you will enjoy yourself just as your father used to do."

It was a conversation Honora remembered after she had gone to bed.

She could not help thinking it would be very difficult to enjoy herself with the Duke unless he paid her a little more attention than he did at the moment.

He had barely spoken a word to her all evening, but she was not aware that this was because her aunt had contrived to keep him away from her.

When he had said good-night, she had thought his eyes looked at her without any admiration in them, and she could sense the waves of resentment coming from him as they had been doing all the evening.

They seemed to intensify when one of the older great-uncles rose to propose a toast to the young couple, and because it was expected of him, the Duke replied.

It was a quite short but witty speech, saying that although he had a large number of relatives of his own, he was quite prepared to add to their numbers.

Although everybody seemed pleased at the compliments he paid the Lang family, Honora was acutely conscious that he was making an effort and there was nothing spontaneous about the pleasant things he said.

The only comfort she had was when her uncle kissed her good-night and told her:

"I was very proud of you tonight, my dear, and there is no doubt that you will do credit to the many beautiful women we have had in our family, and I doubt if any of the Tynemouth Duchesses will rival you."

"Thank you, Uncle George," Honora said simply.

Then, afraid she might be expected to kiss her aunt, she slipped away upstairs.

Only in her own bedroom did she feel safe, sheltered from the Countess's fault-finding and dislike of her, which she made no pretence of concealing.

* * *

The following day there were more things to buy and more relations to meet.

The not-so-important ones had been asked to tea, and because both the Earl and the Duke were in attendance at Buckingham Palace, there was no dinner-party that evening.

Honora had been afraid that she might have an uncomfortable dinner with her aunt, but to her relief the Countess said she intended to have dinner in bed.

No-one suggested she should do the same, so she ate a

small, quick meal downstairs in the Dining-Room, and would have felt very lonely had not Dalton talked to her of her father while he served the meal.

'It is extraordinary,' Honora thought, 'all the nice things everybody says about Papa.'

She wondered if the Duke's relatives and servants would be equally warm-hearted about him.

She very much doubted it, because she was quite sure they were as frightened of him as she was, and she was apprehensive of meeting him again when they were to arrive at Tyne Castle.

When Honora thought about the Castle, she expected it to be rather austere, with a tower.

What she did not know was that it was one of the finest and most historic Castles in England and had been the ancestral home of the Tynes since the days of the Normans.

The building had of course been modernised and enlarged all down the centuries, and the third Duke had in Georgian times spent a fortune on the interior.

He had employed the greatest architects not only to alter the rooms and their decoration but also to design the furniture for the State-Rooms.

This, according to the Countess, had made it immeasurably finer than anything the Queen could boast of at Windsor.

Honora was to find that her aunt always seemed to speak as if the Castle belonged to her, and to point out how it was superior in every way to anything possessed by anyone else.

As usual she made sure that Honora appreciated what was being done for her.

"I see you have been given the Queen's Room," she said when they arrived. "I hope you know enough history to be aware that Queen Elizabeth stayed here when she was a girl, and again when she was on the throne."

As Honora obviously had no idea of this, her aunt sneered:

"I cannot think what they taught you in that expensive School, but I suppose, being foreigners and of course jealous of the British, they played down our achievements by cracking up their own."

Honora longed to say that the teachers had actually taught her the history of every important country in Europe, but she knew that to say so would be a mistake.

The Countess went on:

"Try to make a few intelligent remarks about the Castle— not to the Duke, for he will not listen to you, but his family will be only too ready to say he should have married somebody with more brains."

She did not wait for Honora's answer but left the bedroom in a manner which told her she was contemptuous of everything her niece could do.

Honora did not understand, and fortunately because she was so young and innocent it never crossed her mind that the Countess was suffering agonies in knowing that another woman would fill the place in the Duke's life that she longed for.

Nevertheless, she was too clever not to make herself anything but charming in the presence of his relatives, and she praised Honora publicly, saying that in every way she would make the Duke a very suitable wife.

Only Honora sensed the insincerity of the way she spoke, and it made her feel uneasy and very thankful that her uncle was there.

"Help me, Uncle George," she said as they went down to dinner the first night. "I am frightened of these strange people who are looking at me as if I were a freak in a Circus."

The Earl laughed.

"Not a freak, my dear."

"That is what I feel like," Honora said, "and now I know exactly what the 'Bearded Lady' feels, and perhaps the calf with six legs."

The Earl laughed again.

"How can you know about such things?"

"When I was in Florence I read a book which described King George IV's Coronation and the fête that took place in Hyde Park, where there was a huge Circus and a number of very strange side-shows."

"If you talk to your future relatives in such a way," the Earl answered, "I am sure they will be scandalised!"

"I am trying to appear brave," Honora confessed, "but I really am very frightened."

"Just stay close to me, and leave the Duke's relatives to your aunt. She is much more capable of coping with them than you and I are."

When the Earl spoke to her like that, Honora thought it was almost like having her father with her again.

Therefore, when she went into the Drawing-Room she was smiling, and many of the people there thought she looked like a breath of spring.

Again there were a great many congratulations and good wishes to listen to, and again there were toasts and another speech from the Duke.

When dinner was over, most of the guests sat down at the card-tables, and just as Honora thought the Duke was coming across the room to speak to her, her aunt said:

"I presume you can play the piano?"

"Yes, Aunt Aline."

"Then go and play it, but softly, so that it will not disturb those playing Bridge. It will give you something to do."

Obediently Honora went to the large piano which stood in an alcove of the room in which they had gathered after dinner.

It was not the magnificent Drawing-Room where they had first assembled, but a room adjoining it, which Honora was to learn later was always used when the guests wished to play cards.

There were some very fine paintings round the walls, which she told herself she would look at later, and as she sat down on the piano-stool she noticed that the Duke and her aunt were the only two people in the party who were not occupied.

They were talking intimately together, and she only

hoped they were not talking about her and that she had not done something wrong.

Then as she started to play she forgot everything but her enjoyment of the music.

No-one had been interested that she had won the music prize at the School each year she had been there.

Because she was such a good musician, the Mother Superior had insisted on her having extra music lessons rather than waste her time drawing and painting, at which she was not very proficient.

To Honora it was a joy and a delight to be able to play music, which to her Italian teacher was more important in life than eating and drinking.

"Music must not only lift your heart," he had said, "but the hearts of all who listen to you. Therefore, do not play with your fingers but with your soul!"

Because he had spoken so eloquently and Honora understood what he was trying to say, she tried to express her thoughts and her feelings in music, and in the last six months before she left Florence she had begun to compose.

She was far too afraid of being laughed at by the other girls to tell them what she was doing, but she had played one melody to her teacher, who had listened to it intently and said:

"That is a beginning! The mists are clearing away, and if you go on you will find your way to a Paradise which is waiting for all real musicians. It is there that they link their compositions with God."

She was thinking of what he had said now as she played first some classical music, and then, because she was sure nobody was listening, she played the last piece she had composed herself.

Without realising it, she was expressing her fear of the future and her longing for the love that she felt she was now losing—the love she had thought one day she would find with the man she married.

She was concentrating so intently on what she was doing that for the moment, as her fingers rested at the end of a melody that came from the very depths of her being, she was not aware that somebody was standing near the piano.

Then she raised her eyes and gave a little start as she saw the Duke beside her.

For a moment he did not speak. Then he asked:

"Where did you learn to play like that?"

"I-in . . . Florence."

"Of course, I forgot, you were at School there. And is that your composition or somebody else's?"

She was surprised that he should ask the question or have the slightest idea that she was capable of composing anything.

"It is . . . mine," she replied without really thinking, "but I was not aware that . . . anybody was . . . listening."

He smiled at her before he said:

"I will keep your secret."

When he walked away she looked after him in surprise, and as she did so she saw her aunt come back from the door, where she had been speaking to somebody who was leaving.

She put out her hand to touch the Duke on the arm.

She looked up at him as she spoke, and with the candle-light from the chandelier glistening on the huge tiara she wore on her dark hair, she looked exceedingly beautiful.

Then, to Honora's surprise as she watched them, the Duke seemed deliberately to turn away from her aunt while she was still speaking to him.

He walked to the far end of the room, and when he sat down at one of the card-tables, Honora saw by the expression on her aunt's face that she was angry.

She wondered what had gone wrong.

At the same time, she hoped apprehensively that it was nothing to do with her, which might make her aunt even more disagreeable than she was already.

* * *

During the following days at the Castle, she never had a chance to speak to the Duke alone. Not that she really wanted to be with him, but she thought it rather strange that he never attempted to talk to her.

The first morning that she went out riding, her uncle was with her before the Duke joined them. However, they had got only a little way down the drive before two male cousins came riding after them.

Although Honora found it rather exciting to be the only woman in the party, she had the feeling that the Duke was deliberately leaving her to ride beside the Earl, while he talked to the other two men.

It was their last night at the Castle, when most of the other guests had already left, that the Countess exploded her bomb-shell.

"I believe, Ulric," she said to the Duke, "it would be a good idea if you were married the first week of next month."

"Why should you think that?" the Duke asked sharply.

"I cannot help feeling," she explained, "that it would be better both for you and for Honora to be married quickly, rather than have to put up with house-party after house-party, all exactly like the one we had this week."

The way she spoke made Honora look at her in surprise, because she thought it would be impossible for anybody, except someone in the same circumstances as herself, not to enjoy the party which had just taken place.

The Duke, as she had expected, had been a perfect host.

There was everything available for those who wished to be energetic, and for those who did not, there was the Castle itself to interest them, besides delicious meals and various pleasant neighbours invited both for luncheon and for dinner to relieve any monotony for those who were staying in the house.

Her mother had often explained to her how things were done in grand houses, and she appreciated the enormous number of quiet, well-organised servants there were.

One had only to think of something one wanted for it to be there.

She expected that the Duke would now tell her aunt

that she must be excessively critical to find fault with what had seemed perfection—a superb performance to rival even the most polished production on the stage.

To her surprise, he said instead:

"I should have thought there was no hurry, but if that is what you want..."

"I am only thinking of you," the Countess said softly, "and I had not realised until now how many relations we both have, all of whom are determined to have their 'pound of flesh'!"

"They are certainly making sure of that!" the Duke agreed. "I have had a dozen letters from cousins I did not even know existed who wish to be invited to stay."

"There you are!" the Countess exclaimed. "George and I have had exactly the same experience. I think if I hear one more tiresome woman asking me if I really think you will be happy, I shall scream!"

The Earl looked up from the newspaper he was reading.

"They could hardly expect you to say that the bride and bridegroom would be unhappy!"

To Honora, listening, there was a barely perceptible little pause before her aunt said in the insincere tone she had grown to recognise:

"No, of course not, and of course I said they would be divinely happy!"

Because Honora could not bear to listen to any more, knowing that her intuition was now concerned with herself, and not liking what she was hearing, she rose.

Without being asked, she went into the next room, leaving the door open.

If she just disappeared, she thought, her uncle and aunt might think it rude, so she just did what she wished to do, like everybody else in the party, and sat down at the piano.

Only by playing music did she feel she could escape from the questions that kept asking themselves in her brain and from the feeling that she was being carried down a torrent in a vessel over which she had no control.

She had been playing for some minutes when she heard

footsteps, and she knew before he came to the piano that it was the Duke who had come to her from the Drawing-Room.

She was also aware that he had shut the door behind him.

He came to the piano, and although she did not stop playing, she made the sound a little softer.

"I wanted to see you, Honora," he said, "for I am sure you must think me very remiss for not having given you an engagement-ring before now."

Because that had never crossed Honora's mind, she stopped playing and looked at him in surprise.

"An engagement-ring?"

"It is usual," the Duke replied drily. "I have one for you that has been in my family for many years. Your aunt told me your size, and I have had it altered."

Honora did not speak, but she saw that he held in his hand a small velvet box.

Putting it down on the piano in front of her, he opened it, and as he did so Honora saw that the box contained a diamond ring which was certainly very beautiful.

One very large diamond in the centre was surrounded by a circle of smaller diamonds, which made it very impressive. But after a swift look at it she thought that it was so large that she wondered if she could really wear it.

"This ring," the Duke said, looking down at it, "has a history which I am sure my Curator would enjoy telling you. In fact, it figures in several of the books about the family."

"Thank you very much," Honora said automatically.

"I suppose conventionally," the Duke said, "I should put it on your finger."

Honora held out her hand.

As she did so, she remembered her mother saying:

"When your father gave me my engagement-ring, it was not a very large one, because he was very hard-up at the time, but to me it was the most marvellous jewel in the whole world and had a magic about it which it has never lost."

She smiled as she looked back at the past, saying

"I think what thrilled me even more than the ring was that your father kissed my finger a dozen times, and then the ring, before he put it on and said:

"'This is one of the chains with which I intend to bind you to me for life.'"

Honora remembered giving a little cry.

"Oh, Mama, how romantic! I can imagine Papa saying lovely things like that."

"He always says lovely things to me," her mother had replied in a soft voice.

"I hope it fits," the Duke said, bringing Honora's mind back to the present.

"Yes, perfectly, thank you."

"I am pleased you like it," he said briskly. "My mother was the last person to wear it, and she always believed it was a very lucky ring."

"I hope that is what it will be for me," Honora said, looking down at her hand.

However, she did not think the Duke had heard her, for he had opened the door and walked back into the Drawing-Room where she thought her aunt was waiting for him.

The preparations for the wedding filled everybody's mind and conversation for the next three weeks, until Honora felt there could be nothing left to say.

Every night at dinner-parties the people talked about it, and every day she was occupied with fittings and shopping for her trousseau.

Sometimes her uncle took her driving with him, or, because she begged him to do so, he rode with her either in Hyde Park when they were in London or in the country at Langstone Hall.

They were not entertained again at the Castle, and the reason for this, although Honora did not know it, was that her aunt could not bear to think of her being fawned upon as their future hostess by the Duke's relatives and friends.

She had seen it happen all too clearly on their first visit and realised that she had been brushed to one side as unimportant.

In the future Honora would be the Duchess who would

invite the Duke's friends to the Castle, and they therefore wanted to make certain that they ingratiated themselves and would not be forgotten.

The idea made the Countess want to scream with fury, but years of scheming to get her own way had taught her not only how to act but also how to control her feelings.

"There are so many people in our County who want to meet the future bride and bridegroom," she said to the Earl, "that I have no intention of boring myself by staying at the Castle again until after the wedding is over."

He had looked at her in surprise.

"You always told me how much you enjoyed the Duke's home," he said. "In fact, you have in the past compared it rather unfavourably with mine."

"I find it uncomfortable," the Countess said.

Then, because she felt the Earl found it hard to believe her, she said in the caressing tone which always captivated him:

"I am not envious, darling, of anything anybody else has. You have given me everything I could possibly desire. Langstone House is home to me, and that is where I want to be."

The Earl was delighted.

After that the weekend parties took place in Buckinghamshire, but to Honora they were very little different from those at the Castle.

There were still people pouring in for every meal, all relations of some sort, and she never had a chance of speaking to the Duke alone, even though she was actually beginning to think it was something she would like to do.

'I am sure there are things we should talk about,' she thought as their marriage drew nearer and nearer, 'and I should get to know him.'

But how she could do that when they never sat next to each other at meals, and her aunt seemed always to be guiding him away from wherever she was going, she was not sure.

He went riding with her and her uncle when they were in Buckinghamshire, but he never joined them in London,

and in the country he would often ride ahead or jump high
fences which her uncle would not allow her to attempt.

"I like jumping, Uncle George," she protested.

"Then get the Duke when he is your husband to lower
the jumps on his private race-course," the Earl had answered.
"At the moment they are too high for any woman."

Honora wanted to reply that she was determined if she
got the chance to try the jumps as they were, and was
certain, despite her uncle's apprehension, that they would
not be too high for her.

She had ridden with her father since the time she could
walk, and although their horses were not as well bred or
expensive as either the Earl's or the Duke's, she was quite
certain that no jump would be too high, nor was she
frightened of them.

Because she found that her aunt disapproved of almost
everything she said and snubbed her openly, she had
learnt to say very little.

She thought a little wistfully that she would like to talk
to the Duke and find out what interested him.

She had not forgotten that he had asked her if she
composed, and he had not seemed surprised when she
had told him that she could.

"Perhaps he is musical," she said to herself, "and that at
least would be one point in his favour."

She was not certain what the others might be, but she
had the uncomfortable feeling that there were very few of
them.

She had seen his enormous Library at the Castle and
was aware that the books had been collected over the
centuries, but she had not liked to ask him if he himself
enjoyed reading.

She would also have liked to discuss with him what
were his special interests in Parliamentary affairs.

She studied the newspaper reports of debates in the
House of Lords to see if he had made a speech, but she
could not find one and thought perhaps that was because
he was so involved with getting married.

Now that she was back in England, she read the newspapers very carefully every day.

Although they had lived in a small, unimportant village, her mother and father had always kept up with what was happening in the Political World and especially with the controversies concerning Reforms which could affect country life.

She was sure the Duke knew a lot about this since he owned so many Estates, but once again it was impossible to ask him about it because they were never alone.

Every day her trousseau grew larger and larger, and she began to think she would never live long enough to wear all the gowns her aunt had bought for her.

It seemed as if she was feverishly spending money in a way that Honora could not understand.

She thought the Duke would have the idea that she was extremely extravagant if he saw the number of trunks she would have to take away with her from Langstone House.

"What is the point of so many gowns," she asked herself despairingly, "when he is not likely to admire me in even one of them?"

* * *

At the Ball given by the Duchess of Richmond, the Duke of Tynemouth and the Countess of Langstone moved nonchalantly from the Ball-Room into the garden.

Without speaking, they walked through the shadows of the trees which were decorated with Chinese lanterns and beyond the lights where few of the dangers had penetrated.

"This is driving me mad!" the Duke said, breaking their silence.

"I know," the Countess said caressingly, "it has been maddening both for you and for me, but there is nothing we can do about it."

"The whole thing is unnatural and a dead bore!"

"I agree with you, but after your marriage it will be better."

"Why should you think that?"

"Because, dearest, there will be no more of this formal and necessary entertaining, and once your honeymoon is over, we will be able to see each other without any difficulty."

There was silence, and what the Duke was thinking was so obvious that Aline said quickly:

"There is no need to worry about Honora. You can leave her in the country or in London, whichever you like, and we can have quiet little parties with our real friends, and we will be together as it is impossible to be at this moment."

"If I have to drink one more toast or make one more damned silly speech," the Duke said, "I will chuck the whole thing up and go abroad."

There was a little silence. Then Aline said in a very soft voice:

"How can you be so cruel when I am thinking only of you? And, darling man, have you thought what you might be doing at this moment in Saxe-Coburg?"

"I know! I know!" the Duke said derisively. "But the whole thing is like a very bad play which will not come to an end, and I have no intention of going on much longer."

"You have to, for both our sakes," Aline said softly.

As they were speaking she had been drawing him without his being aware of it into one of the arbours that had been arranged in various parts of the garden.

This one was in shadow, and instead of sitting down on the seat with its soft cushions, she moved close to the Duke and put her arms round his neck.

He kissed her roughly and almost angrily, as if he was relieving his feelings rather than enjoying what he was doing.

Then as Aline drew closer and still closer to him, his kisses became more passionate.

She knew that once again she had swept away his depression and the rebellion which she had sensed was not very far from the surface.

It was a long time later that they walked slowly back to join the crowds moving under the trees and return to the Ball-Room.

As they did so, the Countess enjoyed a sense of triumph that once again she had held the Duke captive, and no-one, not even his wife, would be able to take him from her.

Chapter Five

*H*onora looked out the window and saw it was a lovely day for her wedding.

The sun was shining, the flowers were a kaleidoscope of colour in the garden, and the flags on top of the marquee where the tenants and Estate workers were to celebrate were moving only very slightly in the soft breeze.

It would prevent anybody from feeling too hot, she thought, and all the windows of the Ball-Room where the Reception was to be held would be open.

For the last few days she had felt as if she moved in a dream, and now that the day of the wedding had actually come, she could not believe it was real.

There had been so much to do, and her aunt had become more disagreeable and more vitriolic every moment, so that only by shutting herself away in a fantasy-world could Honora ignore the future which was looming nearer and nearer.

When she did think about it she was frightened, but fortunately when she went to bed at night she was too tired to do anything but fall asleep.

Now she found herself wondering if at the last moment she should run away.

She could imagine the consternation it would cause and the row that would ensue, but at the same time she would be free—free to be herself and not just the Duke's wife.

She could not think of herself as a Duchess. She would merely be one of his possessions, with, as far as he was concerned, as much freedom as if she were a chair or a table.

'If I were a horse he would pay more attention to me,' she thought several times.

But she felt too shy to force herself upon the Duke and try to talk to him.

Anyway, it would have been impossible because whenever the Duke came to the house, her aunt always seemed to find something for her to do which involved her going either upstairs or to the garden or the stables.

Innocently, Honora had explained this to herself by supposing that her aunt was frightened that she might once again tell the Duke that she had no wish to marry him.

"What would be the point when I have no choice except to do as I am told?" she asked herself ruefully.

Now, at the very last moment, she wondered if she dared disappear and deprive the wedding of the bride.

Then she knew she had nowhere to go, and, what was more, she was quite certain her aunt would have her brought back.

She would also doubtless explain her absence by pretending that she had been taken ill, and the arrangements for her marriage would be made all over again.

'There is nothing I can do,' she thought despairingly, and could only send out a prayer to her mother and father to help her.

She was praying all the way as she drove with her uncle to the Church. She knew from the number of invitations her aunt had sent out that it would be packed to bursting, but what she had not expected was the huge crowd of sightseers from the village and the Estate who were waiting outside.

Her uncle's closed carriage was drawn by horses wearing flowers on their heads, their manes plaited with white ribbons, and as she stepped from it loud cheers broke out.

Women touched her for luck and cried: "God bless you, dearie!" or, "You'll be happy with th' handsomest man who ever walked this earth!"

The village women were not the only ones who admired the Duke.

Honora had been aware of the fulsome compliments her relatives had paid him, and as they kept telling her how lucky she was, she could hear the genuine admiration in their voices and see a look almost of adulation in their eyes.

"He should be marrying somebody who feels like that about him," she told herself a hundred times.

While she had to admit that he was exceedingly handsome, that he rode magnificently, and that from what she had heard he was also intelligent, she had had no chance of learning of any other qualities he might have.

Because her aunt was always telling her how stupid she was and found fault with everything she did, she wondered if she spoke of her in the same way to the Duke.

"If we are to be even remotely happy," Honora reasoned, "we shall have to talk to each other about other things besides our wedding, and I wish I knew what interests him besides horses."

Because she felt it was important, she had taken the trouble to read the sporting-pages of the newspapers every day and to learn the names of other race-horse owners.

She had tried to ask a few questions of her uncle, but she realised immediately that not only had the Earl no wish to talk about the Duke, but, as she had thought before, he disliked him.

It seemed strange, considering what a close friend he appeared to be of both her uncle and her aunt, but she was too shy to ask the Earl point-blank what he thought.

Instead, the conversation always seemed to get round to her father, which from her point of view was far more interesting and enjoyable.

However, she was very careful not to mention either her mother or her father in front of her aunt.

She was by now quite accustomed to the scathing remarks the Countess made about the debts her father had left behind him and the opportunities he had missed by not making a good marriage.

"Anyway," she had said, "you will make up for his deficiencies on that score, and do not forget that as a Duchess you should spend a great deal of time looking after the poor on your husband's Estate and also visiting Hospitals, Orphanages, and Schools."

As she had repeated this several times, Honora hoped that once she was married, her aunt would not organise her life in the same way as she was doing now.

"I need to have time to read, to think, and to... talk to... the Duke," Honora told herself.

She was not quite sure why she felt it was so important that they should talk to each other.

But she was horrified even by the idea of spending the rest of her life surrounded by people having parties every night and still being an outsider because she could not share their jokes or their memories.

"I will run away!" Honora said aloud.

As she did so, she thought that it would then be too late for the Queen to insist on the Duke marrying Princess Sophie.

Anyway, there would have to be a decent interval before he could become engaged for the second time.

The door opened and her aunt's sharp voice startled her as she said:

"I am going to the Church now. You have five minutes. Do not keep us waiting."

'It is too late,' Honora thought, and in exactly five minutes she obediently went down the stairs.

The cheers of the crowd followed her into the cool dimness of the ancient Church.

It had been enlarged at the same time as her grandfather had redecorated the house.

Nearly all the guests had somehow managed to be seated, with the exception of a number of tall, good-looking ushers who had shown them to their seats.

One of them smiled at Honora as she entered the Church, and because there was no mistaking the admiration in his eyes, she somehow felt a little comforted and was not so nervous.

Nevertheless, she held on tightly to her uncle's arm as they moved slowly up the aisle to where the Duke was waiting for her at the chancel steps.

As she stood beside him, Honora was vividly conscious that once again he was hating her and resenting the part he had to play of being a bridegroom.

Although she tried to pray, she found it hard to think of anything but the feelings of the man beside her.

He put the wedding-ring on her finger, and as he did so she knew that he was almost at the point of refusing to go on with it.

If she had wanted to run away, so had he, and she wished she could have talked to him beforehand, so that they could perhaps have made an arrangement by which they both could have escaped.

It was too late now, for the Bishop had given them his blessing and they were moving into the vestry to sign the Register.

"I am married! I am married!" Honora kept telling herself, and she thought the Duke must be saying the same thing.

She could feel his resentment vibrating from him almost like streaks of lightning.

Then somebody, she was not sure who it was, raised her veil and drew it back over the diamond tiara her aunt had lent her.

"I suppose," she had said grudgingly, "you could have had some of the Tynemouth tiaras to choose from. There are certainly enough of them. But the Langs would think it strange, and my jewels are quite as good as theirs."

It did not seem worth making a fuss about it one way or the other, Honora thought, but she was too wise to say so.

Instead, she knew that despite her feelings she looked exactly as everybody would expect a bride to look, except that her gown was more sensational than what most brides could afford, and the jewels on her head and round her neck glittered like a constellation of stars.

Then, having spoken not one word, she was walking down the aisle on the Duke's arm.

Once again as they came out into the Church porch there were cheers, while rose-petals were thrown at them and on the path in front of them.

Because it was traditional, her aunt had arranged that they should drive back to the house in an open carriage.

Now the children from the village ran alongside it as they drove along the oak-lined avenue, and there were more employees to wave as they passed.

It took only a few minutes to reach the house, where the servants helped Honora to alight, and she and the Duke walked down the corridor which led to the Ball-Room.

Because Honora had no friends in England, her aunt had dispensed with bridesmaids, and to help her move more quickly one of the footmen lifted up her short train.

This made it difficult for her to say anything to the Duke, and by the time they reached the Ball-Room, her aunt and uncle, who had followed them in another carriage, were already there.

They had entered the house by a side-door to reach the position where they would receive their quests.

An hour later Honora began to think that her hand would drop off from all the hand-shakes she had received, and she was also surprised at the number of strange people who kissed her.

If people were over-affectionate towards her, it was nothing to what the Duke was enduring, and she could hear those he greeted cooing at him in caressing tones.

It was her uncle who brought her a glass of champagne, saying as he did so:

"You must be feeling exhausted, my dear, and it is almost time to cut the cake."

It was then that Honora glanced at the Duke and saw by the expression on his face that he was longing to get away.

Her aunt had told her, in her usual sharp voice which brooked no argument, that she was to change her clothes immediately after they had cut the cake.

"I have not asked where we are going when we leave here," Honora had said.

For some reason which she could not understand, she knew that the question made her aunt even more annoyed than she was already.

"You are staying tonight in London. Then doubtless after that Ulric will inform you of his plans."

Honora found it surprising that her aunt did not know, but again she was aware that it would be unwise to ask too many questions.

However, she was glad that they would not have too long a journey, as London was only two hours' drive from Langstone Hall.

The cake which had been laboriously cooked by her uncle's Chef was cut with a sword, somebody proposed their health, and the Duke replied with a few words.

Then Honora found herself being piloted upstairs by the Countess to where Emily, who had been chosen to go with her on her honeymoon as a lady's-maid, was waiting.

"Now hurry up! You know it is always a mistake to keep a man waiting!" the Countess said sharply, and went from the bedroom, leaving Honora and Emily alone.

"You looked lovely, Miss—I mean—Your Grace!" Emily exclaimed. "Everyone's a-sayin' there's never been such a beautiful bride."

"I am glad they thought so," Honora replied.

However, she was thinking that there was certainly one person who did not think so, if he had even noticed her at all, and that was the man who was now her husband.

When she thought about him, it was as if there were a lump inside her breast that grew heavier and heavier as she changed her clothes.

The moment had now come when she would be alone with the Duke and his dislike and resentment of her.

"Help me, Papa," she murmured beneath her breath.

"Did you say somethin', Your Grace?" Emily enquired.

"I was only talking to myself," Honora replied. "Give me my bonnet, Emily. We must not keep the horses waiting."

"You'll be in London long afore I am, Your Grace, with the 'orses you're travelling with."

Honora looked surprised, and Emily asked:

"Didn't you know 'is Grace is takin' you in 'is Phaeton?"

"I had no idea, but I am very glad," Honora answered. "It will be pleasant to be out in the open air rather than cooped up in a carriage."

She thought with relief that it would also preclude the necessity of talking to the Duke.

She had the feeling that at the moment it was the last thing she wished to do, although it was something she had wanted before.

She felt that he would be even more incensed than he had been before at having to drive away from his friends and relations with a strange woman whom he had married only to escape from a German Princess.

'Perhaps once we are alone it will be easier to get to know him,' Honora thought.

At the same time, she was aware of the feeling in her breast, which was heavy and depressing, and her lips felt dry.

It was then, as she was just finishing tying the ribbons under her chin, that her aunt came back into the room.

"Are you ready?" she enquired. "You are taking long enough about it!"

"I have been as quick as I could, Aunt Aline."

"You go now, Emily," the Countess said. "You will find the brake waiting for you, and I shall be extremely annoyed if any of the luggage is left behind."

"I'm sure I've remembered everything, M'Lady," Emily replied.

"Then what are you waiting for?"

Emily hurried from the room, and the Countess walked to where Honora was sitting at the dressing-table.

She stood without speaking, and Honora looked at her apprehensively, wondering what she would find wrong with her appearance.

"You are married!" the Countess said at last. "Now, for Heaven's sake, do not bore the Duke with protestations of affection, and do not plead with him, which is something he most dislikes."

Honora was surprised, and as her aunt apparently wished her to say something, she murmured:

"N-no . . . of course not."

"The sooner you give him a child, the better!" the Countess went on. "He has to have an heir, but there will be no need for you to be over-dramatic about it."

As she had nothing more to say, she swept to the door and therefore did not see the look of consternation on Honora's face or the apprehension in her eyes.

* * *

Only when they had left Langstone House and were travelling at an incredible pace behind a team of four perfectly matched horses did she remember what her aunt had said, and she found it almost incredible.

Because of the haste in which they had been married and because she had never before been alone with the Duke, it had never struck her for one moment that she would be expected to give him children at once.

"How can we be intimate until we know each other very much better than we do at the moment?" she asked herself.

She had no idea how a woman had a baby.

It was something which had never been discussed at the Convent, and when her mother had died Honora was still too young to ask her such questions which had not then concerned her in any way.

As they drove on, the Duke concentrated on his horses, and as the countryside flashed past them Honora thought that her aunt was speaking about something that would happen only perhaps months or years later.

'After all, he has never even kissed me,' she thought, 'and surely he will not . . . touch me until he has ceased to . . . hate me and we have become . . . friends!'

This seemed so reasonable that when, after they had driven for nearly an hour, the Duke asked: "You are all right?" Honora was able to reply quite naturally:

"Yes, of course, and I am so glad we are driving like this and not in a closed carriage."

"It is something I find intolerable at any time," the Duke replied. "The only thing that could have prevented us from reaching London as quickly as we shall do now is if it had been pouring with rain."

"Then I am very glad it is such a lovely day," Honora said, "and your horses are superb."

"They are a team I bought six months ago," the Duke replied. "They were expensive, but worth every penny I paid for them!"

"I am sure they are."

They drove on in silence, and now she told herself that her fears were groundless. The Duke was treating her casually and not as if she was a bride.

When they arrived at Tynemouth House in Park Lane, she found that the staff were lined up to greet them, and after Honora had shaken hands with everybody from the Butler to the lowest kitchen-boy, the Duke said:

"Would you like a glass of champagne, or would you prefer to go straight to your room?"

"I would like to go to my room," Honora replied.

She felt that he was relieved at her decision, and the Housekeeper, looking very much like Mrs. Morton in rustling black silk, escorted her up the stairs.

Her room was very impressive, with a huge four-poster bed carved and gilded and with curtains of blue silk.

"This has always been the Duchess's room," the Housekeeper explained.

"It is very lovely!" Honora answered. "Will you tell me your name?"

"I'm Mrs. Barnes, and I hope Your Grace'll be comfortable. Beatrice, one of the maids here, will look after you until Your Grace's lady's-maid arrives."

"I am afraid that will not be for some time, because I do not believe any horses could travel as fast as His Grace's!"

"I'm sure you are right, Your Grace, and you needn't worry about your gowns, as quite a number came here direct from Bond Street."

Mrs. Barnes opened a wardrobe door as she spoke, and Honora saw that a dozen of the gowns which her aunt had ordered for her trousseau had been sent direct to Tynemouth House.

She had a bath and afterwards put on a very elegant gown that was not unlike the one in which she had been married.

Because Mrs. Barnes expected her to wear white as a bride, she did not argue but allowed herself to be helped into a gown made entirely of lace and ornamented with small bunches of white roses.

"I suppose, Your Grace, your maid will know which of these gowns to take with you on your honeymoon tomorrow?" Mrs. Barnes said.

"H-honeymoon?" Honora repeated. "Are we leaving tomorrow?"

"I understood that was His Grace's intention, and that you're going to his Hunting Lodge in Leicestershire."

Mrs. Barnes smiled before she added:

"It's a very attractive house, Your Grace, and you'll be very comfortable there. The gardens are nearly as beautiful there as they are at the Castle."

"I shall look forward to seeing them," Honora replied, "and I am sure Emily will know what I should take with me."

When she was dressed she walked slowly down the stairs, feeling once again a little frightened.

"I must try to behave naturally," she admonished herself. "It is what Mama would expect, and we cannot go on forever hating and resenting each other because we have been forced to marry in this precipitate way."

This was easier to decide than to put into operation, and she knew when she entered the attractive room where the Duke was waiting for her that she could not help trembling a little.

Because she had been at Tynemouth House for dinner-parties, she realised they were sitting not in the large Drawing-Room but in a much smaller, more comfortable room in which there were a great number of books.

Forgetting the Duke for a moment, she exclaimed:

"Oh, you have a lot of books here! How splendid! I was afraid I would find them only at the Castle."

"These are the books I have bought for myself," the Duke replied.

"Then you do like reading!" Honora exclaimed without thinking.

Then as she saw the question in his eyes she explained:

"It may sound . . . rude, but I have often . . . wondered if all the books at the Castle were chosen by your forebears . . . and you yourself are not much interested in them."

"As it happens, I read a great deal," the Duke replied, "and I suppose from what you have just said that you do too."

"Of course! Books mean so much to me, and especially when I was at School."

She was afraid he might think she was referring to her lesson-books and added quickly:

"I was left behind when the other girls went home for the holidays, and because the Nuns then spent most of their time in prayer, it gave me a great deal of time to read."

She gave him a little smile as she said:

"I am afraid I spent much more than I could afford on buying the books I wanted, but fortunately there was also a Lending Library in Florence, although not a very large one."

The Duke poured her a glass of champagne before he said:

"I shall be interested to see what is your taste in literature."

"It is very varied," Honora replied, "and stretches from Elizabethan poets to the French novelists."

The Duke laughed.

"I can quite see I shall have to have more bookcases added to this room and certainly more than there are already in your *Boudoir*."

"That will be a change from having them where they always were at home—on the floor! Papa and Mama read a lot too, so we always had more books than we could find room for."

"I somehow never thought of your father as being a great reader," the Duke remarked.

"Papa enjoyed everything he did, although it was Mama who encouraged him to read. He preferred books on horses, but we used to have animated discussions on all sorts of other subjects when he was . . . at home."

There was just a slight pause before the last words and the Duke said:

"Did your mother always go with him when he was staying away with friends?"

Honora was quick enough to realise that this was a pertinent question which concerned herself, and she answered truthfully:

"Mama always wanted to go with Papa because she hated being separated from him, but sometimes when there were racing- or hunting-parties, ladies were not invited."

Her voice softened and she finished:

"Then she would be left at home, and she missed him so much that the only way of consoling herself during his absence was to read."

The Duke was just about to say something when dinner was announced and they went into the large Dining-Room where Honora had been before.

The table was decorated with white flowers, and there was a special dinner with a large number of courses which the Chef thought appropriate to the occasion.

Only when the servants were for the moment out of earshot did Honora say in a conspiratorial tone:

"I cannot eat all this!"

"Nor can I," the Duke admitted, "but I suppose we shall have to make an effort."

"Yes, of course, otherwise your Chef would feel hurt."

She looked down at the menu in front of her, which was supported by a gold stand bearing the Duke's monogram, and said:

"I see there is a cake."

The Duke gave a groan. Then he said in a tone of relief:

"At least I shall not have to make a speech after we have cut it!"

Honora laughed.

"I thought the one you made today, and which was the shortest, was the best."

"Because it was the shortest?"

"No, because I admired the way you put everything which had to be said so concisely and so wittily."

The Duke looked at her with what she thought was a twinkle in his eye and said:

"I am gratified by your approval, Honora."

A faint colour came into her cheeks as she said:

"Perhaps . . . you think it . . . impertinent of me to . . . approve or disapprove, but what I said was very sincere."

"I suppose because you have been in a Convent you always tell the truth," the Duke remarked, as if he was working it out for himself.

"I tell the truth because I was brought up to do so," Honora corrected. "Both Papa and Mama hated people who lied, and they always knew, as I do, when someone was lying."

She thought there was a slight frown between the Duke's eyes and wondered if she had said anything wrong.

Then the servants came in with another course from which they must help themselves, and they started to talk of other things.

It was a relief when finally the dinner came to an end and, the Duke having said he did not wish for port, they walked together back to the Sitting-Room in which they had met before dinner.

Honora went at once to look at the book-shelves, recognising many books she had already read and a great number she wished to read.

She walked from shelf to shelf until she suddenly thought that perhaps she was being rude and she should in fact be talking to the Duke.

He had seated himself in a comfortable armchair and had a glass of brandy in his hand.

She moved towards him, saying:

"I am sorry. I am being selfish and thinking about books when I should be trying to amuse you."

"Is that what you have been told to do, or what you wish to do?"

"Mama always said it was very rude not to talk to a guest," Honora replied. Then after a little pause she added: "But you are not my guest, are you? In fact, I suppose . . . I am yours."

"I do not think that is right either," the Duke argued. "After all, I distinctly remember saying today that 'with all my worldly goods I thee endow,' so I presume we share this house. In any case, you should think of it as your home."

"Yes . . . of course," Honora said, "but it feels . . . very strange at the moment."

"You will get used to it," the Duke said lightly, "and doubtless you will soon be telling me of all the improvements you wish to have made."

Honora shook her head.

"I think that is unlikely. I thought the Castle was perfect in every way, and like an exquisitely acted Play in which everybody knew their parts to perfection."

"Including yourself as the Leading Lady?"

There was just a slightly mocking note in his voice, which Honora did not miss.

"If I thought about myself at all while I was there," she replied, "it was as a member of the audience, who had . . . very little part in what was . . . taking place."

"If that was how you felt, then I should apologise."

"No, no! Of course not!" Honora replied quickly. "I was only speaking the truth, and you must realise this is all very strange and unusual to me after being at School for two years and before that living very quietly in the country."

She gave a little sigh as she added:

"I expect I shall make a lot of mistakes, and you must try not to be angry with me."

The Duke looked at her as if he was about to say something. Instead he glanced at the clock and remarked:

"It is growing late and you have had a very long day. I think, Honora, you should go to bed."

As if he had given her an order, Honora rose to her feet, and he added:

"I shall not be long!"

For one moment she thought she could not have heard him a-right.

Then as he opened the door for her and she went out into the Hall, everything her aunt had said to her came rushing back into her mind.

She knew with a sense of horror that seemed to seep through her that the Duke intended to come to her room and give her a baby, although she had no idea what that entailed.

'He must not do such a thing!' she thought, and turned her head, intending to go back into the room and tell him so.

Then somehow she realised in a way she never had before that she was his wife. She must behave as he expected her to, and there was no-one to help her, no way in which she could escape!

'He cannot do this, he must not!' she thought frantically.

Once again she felt as if there were a heavy weight within her breast, and it was impossible to think.

Instinctively her feet carried her towards the staircase, and as she reached it she saw lying on a chair the cloak which she had brought with her in the Phaeton, but which it had been too warm to wear.

She supposed it had been left there for the morning, when they would be leaving for Leicestershire. As she looked at it an idea came to her.

She had to think, she had to consider what to do about tonight and what she could say to the Duke.

It was almost as if the walls of the house were closing in on her, creating a prison from which she could never escape and in which she lost her identity so completely that she was no longer herself.

'I must think...I must...think!' she thought desperately.

She picked up the cloak and put it over her shoulders, then walked to the front door.

When she reached it she realised that the footman in attendance was looking at her in surprise.

"Please open the door!" she said quickly.

"Do you want a carriage, Your Grace?"

"No, thank you."

The door was opened, and she walked outside and down the steps to the pavement.

Just across the road was the Park, and she thought she would go sit under the trees and think about what she should do.

It would be easier to think in the open than in the house, where the Duke was intending to come up to her bedroom at any moment and perhaps would not listen to what she had to tell him.

There was no traffic about and she crossed the road, but only when she reached the pavement on the other side did she see the iron railings that surrounded the Park.

She knew there were gates which led into it, but she was not certain whether they were open at night. However, she walked down Park Lane, thinking that when she came to the gates she would find whether they were open or closed.

As she walked she was turning over and over in her mind what her aunt had said, and hearing the Duke remark in what she thought was a dry tone:

"I will not be long!"

Quite suddenly she was arrested by a woman's voice saying furiously:

"'Ere, wot d'you think you're doin' of? This be my beat, an' you've no right on it!"

Honora came to a standstill.

She saw facing her a woman who she thought looked very strange, until she realised it was because her face was painted. She had pink cheeks, eye-lashes black with thick mascara, and a crimson mouth.

She looked so different from anybody Honora had ever seen before that for a moment she could only stand and stare at her.

Then as her eyes went to the gaudy feathered bonnet she wore and the crimson cloak trimmed with cheap fur, she said:

"I . . . I am sorry . . . but I do not understand what you are . . . saying to me."

"Yer understands orl right," the woman said angrily.

Her voice was coarse and she had a cockney accent.

Honora did not reply, and she went on:

"This be where Oi works, so clear off an' find somewhere else, an' be quick abaht it!"

"I . . . I was going into the Park," Honora explained.

"As if yer didn't know it's closed up at night!" the woman said scornfully. "Come on, ignoramus, don' try 'em tricks on me!"

Honora thought the woman must be mad and decided that the best thing she could do would be to cross the road to the other side.

She was just about to do so, when two men came up.

"'Avin' a bit o' trouble, Milly?" one of them asked.

"This 'ere woman's trespassing on my beat!" she said. "I tells 'er she ain't got no right 'ere, but 'er don't seem ter understand plain English!"

The men were dark and rather unpleasant-looking, and as they turned to Honora she said quickly:

"I am sorry if I have done anything . . . wrong. I did not mean to upset . . . anybody. I will go . . . away."

She meant once again to cross the road, but at that moment there was a carriage coming and she had to wait for it to pass.

She did not see the two men look at each other with knowing glances, and one of them said:

"We'll look after yer, me dear, an' prevent yer upsettin' Molly. There's plenty o' other places jus' as good as this."

They caught hold of Honora's arms, and now she was very frightened.

"It is quite all right, thank you," she said. "I will go back from . . . where I . . . came."

"Oi thinks that'd be a mistake," one of the men said.

"So do Oi," the other one agreed. "Yer come along wiv us."

"No! No!" Honora exclaimed. "I do not want to do... that!"

She tried to move away from them, but to her consternation she found there was a man on either side of her, and they were holding on to her arms.

As they held her so that she could not escape from them, a hackney-carriage came down the road and one of them hailed it.

"N-no...please...I have to go...back to my...house!" she said quickly.

They did not seem to hear her, and before she could realise what was happening they had bundled her into the hackney-carriage.

So that she could not escape, they sat one on each side of her and she was sandwiched between them.

As the carriage drove off she said quickly:

"Please... you are making a great... mistake. I live just across the other side of the road, and that is... where I must... return."

"Yer can tell that ter Kate!" one of the men said. "She'll know 'ow to deal wi' the likes o' you!"

"You do not understand," Honora said miserably. "I merely came from my house because I thought I could go into the Park and sit under the trees for a few minutes. They will... worry when I do not... return."

As she spoke she thought that the Duke would think it very strange when he went up to her bedroom to find her gone.

She wondered if the footman would tell him she had left the house and if he would think that even stranger.

She had no idea what the men intended to do with her, and she was so frightened that she had nothing more to say as she sat jammed between them.

She was quite certain that if she screamed or made a fuss the cabman driving the hackney-carriage would take no notice of her.

'What can I...do? What...can I do?' she thought frantically.

She suddenly had an idea and said:

"If it is money you want, take me back and I will pay you whatever you want for doing so."

"We're takin' yer to see Kate, an' that's all there is abaht it," the man said almost as if it was a lesson he had learnt by heart.

"Who is . . . Kate?"

"Yer'll find out when we gets there! An' there ain't no point makin' a fuss, that's fer sure!"

Honora wondered frantically what she should do.

She had a feeling that there was no use in trying any more arguments with these two men, who seemed rather stupid.

She thought that perhaps Kate, whoever she might be, would be intelligent enough to realise that she could not disappear from Tynemouth House without there being a hue and cry for her.

They were driving now through streets bright with lights, and there seemed to be quite a number of people about.

Then as Honora was still wondering whether she should appeal once again to the men who were holding her to all intents and purposes prisoner, the carriage came to a standstill.

She glanced through the window and saw there were two lanterns outside a tall house with steps leading up to a front door which also had a light over it.

The men climbed out of the carriage and one paid the cabman, then with one on each side of her, as if they were afraid she would run away, they walked up the steps.

The front door was ajar and they pushed it open.

As they entered, Honora saw that the house was larger than she would have expected. There was a Hall out of which opened a number of doors, and a staircase leading to the next floor, over the bannisters of which two women were leaning.

One glance at them told her that their faces were painted in the same way that Milly's was, and one of them called out:

"Wot yer got there, Jim?"

"We wants Kate. Fetch 'er for us. Which room's empty?"

"Th' one on the left," the woman replied.

Without saying any more, the men half-pulled, half-propelled Honora, although she was making no effort to resist them, to a door at the side of the Hall.

To her surprise, it seemed to be a bedroom but was quite unlike any she had ever seen before.

The walls were bright pink, and there were large mirrors which reflected and rereflected her image as she came in through the door.

The bed also was draped in pink, but one glance told her that it was a very cheap material, and there was no corola to hold the curtains but a large satin bow attached to a hook over which they were draped.

She stood looking round her while the men waited at the half-open door until there was a voice shouting some instructions to somebody outside, and a moment later a woman came into the bedroom.

She was so amazing that Honora could only stare at her.

She was a large, middle-aged woman, heavily painted in the same way as Molly and the girls on the bannisters.

She was wearing a flamboyant evening-gown with the bodice embroidered with large diamanté, while the skirt was covered with frills caught up with bunches of cheap cotton roses.

Round her neck was a fake diamond necklace, and she wore ear-rings to match it which hung from her ears to her fat shoulders.

Her hair, which was frizzed and curled until it looked almost grotesque, was hennaed, and her voice seemed to echo loudly round the room as she exclaimed:

"Wot the devil 'ave you got here?"

"We fahnd 'er on Molly's patch, Kate, 'avin' an argument, they was. We thinks the best thing, as she's pretty, was to bring 'er 'ere to you."

Kate stood and looked Honora over in a manner which made her feel very uncomfortable.

"P-please . . . let me explain . . ." she began.

"Who are yer? Wot's yer name?" Kate interrupted.

"I am the Duchess of Tynemouth!"

Kate reached out and struck her a sharp slap across the cheek.

"That's a lie for a start," she said, "and Oi wants th' truth!"

Honora found it impossible to breathe or to move, and after a moment she put her hand up to her cheek, feeling it could not be true that this common woman had hit her.

As she did so, the movement made her cloak, which she had clasped at the neck, come undone.

Kate and the two men standing watching her saw the gown she wore underneath it and the pearl bracelet, which had been one of her wedding-presents, round her wrist.

For a moment there was silence. Then Kate commanded:

"Tell me who you are, an' Oi wants the truth this time!"

"It . . . is the . . . truth!" Honora insisted, unable to prevent the tremor in her voice. "I . . . I was . . . m-married this m-morning."

"An' you're walkin' in Park Lane ternight? Yer don't expect me ter believe that, do yer?"

Suddenly the man called Jim gave an exclamation.

"Wait a minnit, Kate!"

He put his hand into his pocket and drew out a newspaper which was protruding from it, opened it, turned over the pages, then passed it to Kate.

She looked down at it, then asked sharply:

"Who did yer say yer was?"

"I . . . am the . . . Duchess of . . . Tynemouth," Honora stammered, afraid she would be struck again.

"An' yer was married this mornin'?"

"Yes."

"Where was yer married?"

"At Langstone House . . . in Buckinghamshire. It is where my uncle and aunt . . . live."

Kate stared at her as if to be quite certain she was telling the truth before she said, reading from the newspaper:

"Wot was the name of the Parson as married yer?"

"The Bishop . . . of Oxford."

Kate looked at her searchingly, at the pearls and diamonds on her wrist and the gown she wore under her cloak.

Then she ordered sharply:

"Wait 'ere!"

Kate and the men went from the room, shutting the door behind them, and Honora, feeling as if her legs would no longer carry her, sat down on the edge of the bed.

As she did so, she realised how foolish she had been to leave the house at night and become involved in anything so sordid.

It had never struck her for one moment that it might be dangerous or that anybody would object to her walking in Hyde Park or sitting under the trees.

She had never been allowed to go out alone in Florence, but that was different, because she had been a School-girl.

When she was staying in Grosvenor Square with her aunt and uncle, she had often slipped out into the gardens in the centre of the Square when she had a moment to herself, although it was rare.

Having lived in the country when she was at home with her father and mother, it was only now that she remembered that the garden in the Square was private, and only the householders had special keys with which to open the gate leading into it.

'I have been so stupid,' she thought with a sigh.

She wondered if Kate would allow her to communicate with the Duke and ask him to come fetch her.

A few minutes later Kate and the two men came back into the room, and she rose to her feet, her eyes very wide and frightened.

"If you're the Duchess of Tynemouth, as yer says yer are," Kate said in her common voice, "then I presooms yer husband'll want yer back wiv him, 'specially as it's his weddin' night!"

The two men sniggered.

Remembering that this was exactly what she had been running away from, Honora felt the colour come into her cheeks, and Kate went on:

"In which case, you'd better write to him an' tell him ter come an' fetch yer."

"May I do that?" Honora asked. "I know he will come at once. I realise now that it was very . . . foolish of me to . . . leave the house as . . . I did."

"Wot your husband thinks abaht it ain't none o' my business," Kate answered, "but I'm sure he'll be ever so grateful to us fer lookin' after you."

The way she spoke made Honora stare at her before she asked:

"Are you . . . holding me to . . . ransom?"

Jim laughed before he said:

"She's sharper than we gives 'er credit for, even if 'er didn't know wot Molly was talkin' abaht!"

"You keep yer mouth shut!" Kate said rudely. "Yes, Duchess, you're bein' held ter ransom, an' you can only hope your 'ubby'll pay up fer you. Otherwise, you'll have to stay with me!"

Jim sniggered again, but Kate ignored him.

Honora noticed now that she was holding in her hand a tray on which was a piece of writing-paper, a bottle of ink, and a pen.

She set it down on a table that stood in a corner of the room covered with a pink cloth that was spotted with marks from glasses, and said:

"Now then, you write to yer 'ubby an' tell him to come and fetch you quickly, an' explain that after all the trouble an' expense we've gone to, we wants three hundred pounds to let yer go!"

"Three hundred pounds!" Honora exclaimed.

"Why not five hundred?" Jim questioned. "After all, it's 'is weddin' night!"

"You're right!" Kate exclaimed. "Wiv all them race-'orses he's got, he can well afford five hundred pounds, if not a thousand!"

"Oh, please . . ." Honora begged, "do not ask too much money! He will never have such a large sum with him."

She was worried that she might have to spend the night in this horrible place.

"That sounds reasonable," Kate answered. "Make it five hundred. Gent'men has that sort o' money in th' house."

Honora thought miserably that there was no point in arguing any further and had a frantic desire to get away.

She was frightened of the strange spectacle that Kate made, of Jim and the other man, and of the girls with their painted faces.

She could see them occasionally peeping round the door when they thought Kate was not looking.

The ink was thin and not very black, and the pen was very scratchy, but finally she managed to write:

> I am sorry for being so foolish, but I have been captured by two men and brought here. They say if you will pay them five hundred pounds for the trouble I have caused, you can come to collect me.
>
> I am writing this letter to beg you to come as quickly as you can.
>
> I am very, very sorry.
>
> *Honora.*

Almost before she had finished signing her name, Kate snatched the letter and began to read it slowly.

"That oughta squeeze the money out o' a heart of stone!" she laughed.

She handed it back to Honora, saying:

"Address it!"

There appeared to be no envelope, so Honora folded the paper, turned it over, and addressed it:

> *His Grace the Duke of Tynemouth,*
> *Tynemouth House,*
> *Park Lane.*

She then handed it to Kate, who went from the room, talking to the two men in whispers as she did so.

Then, as if as an after-thought, she came back, picked up the tray with the ink and pen on it, and went out again.

Honora had the idea that they too were writing a letter

to the Duke, and she wondered what they were saying to him.

Then as if she was almost past thinking about it she put her hand up to her forehead, wondering if the Duke would be very angry when he received her letter.

The door opened and one of the girls she had seen peering over the bannisters peeped in. She was wearing a transparent nightgown and over it a rather dirty wrap.

"Yer're a real Duchess, are yer?" she said. "I've seen Dukes, but never a Duchess afore. Yer looks too young."

Honora found herself smiling.

"I only became one this morning."

"Now if Oi was a Duchess," the girl went on, "Oi shouldn't be walking abaht gettin' meself involved wi' Molly. 'Ers like as not t' scratch yer eyes out! She's got th' temper o' wild cat."

"I cannot understand why she was so... annoyed with me," Honora said.

"Oi tell yer why..." the girl began.

At that moment there was a loud voice shouting in the Hall behind her, and she gave a start and said:

"That's Lord Roxton! Oi thought 'e'd be along ternight."

Without saying any more, she shut the door, and Honora stared after her.

She could hear voices being raised outside as somebody walked past the door. She had a sudden fear that Lord Roxton, or whoever it was, would come into the room and find her there.

She was quite certain that the Duke would not want his friends or anybody else to learn how stupid she had been in leaving the house at night and becoming involved with people who were asking ransom money for her.

After a little while the noise of voices stopped and there was silence again.

"How could I have been so foolish?" Honora asked herself.

The question kept repeating itself over and over in her mind until what seemed to be hours later the door of the bedroom opened again.

Chapter Six

When Honora had left the Sitting-Room, the Duke had poured himself some more brandy.

As he drank it he felt a little of the resentment and irritation he had been feeling all day begin to melt away.

He also acknowledged that dinner with his new wife had not been such a bore as he had expected, and she was certainly very lovely.

If he had not realised that himself, everybody he had spoken to had eulogised over Honora's beauty until he had found it difficult, because of his resentment over the wedding, not to argue with them.

Only now, almost against his will, he conceded that if he had to take a wife ready-made for him, Honora was everything she should be, and tonight he had found her to be intelligent.

The mere thought that he had a wife was enough to revive the resentment he had felt when he drove to the Church with his Best Man and found himself hating the ceremony that was waiting for him as he had hated it ever since he awoke that morning.

He had not slept well, and very early he had risen to walk to the window and look out at the mist round the trees in the Park and the first rays of the sun sweeping away the last remaining stars.

He had a yearning, even as Honora had had, to run away, to disappear at the last moment and leave the wedding without a bridegroom.

Then he knew that was impossible, for, whatever his

feelings, he had to behave like a gentleman and as befitted his position at Court.

At the same time, he was man enough to despise himself for being forced into doing something quite contrary to his inclination instead of insisting on his independence.

'This is the price I pay for my title,' he thought bitterly.

The same bitterness seemed to make everything he thought seem ugly, and when he had put the ring on Honora's finger he had felt it was a shackle which made him a prisoner for the rest of his life.

He realised now that without being aware of it he had finished his glass of brandy, and he played with the idea of having another one.

Then he told himself he had never been a hard drinker and was certainly not going to start now.

Almost as if his years of training and self-control forced him to behave like a soldier going into battle, he put down his empty glass, squared his shoulders, and walked towards the door.

It was his wedding-night, and whatever the future held, it was important that he should start his marriage in the correct manner and his wife should have no reason to complain about him.

He opened the door and walked into the Hall.

There he saw to his surprise that the front door was open, and he thought it was a strange time of night for anybody to be calling.

But there was no carriage outside, only a footman standing in the doorway, looking out over the low wall and strip of garden which separated the house from the pavement in Park Lane.

The man did not move, and after a moment as the Duke reached the bottom of the stairs he asked:

"What are you waiting for, James?"

The footman started and turned back into the Hall, saying:

"I were waiting, Your Grace, for Her Grace to return."

The Duke thought he could not have understood him.

He had always thought James a rather stupid young man, and now he asked:

"What are you talking about? Her Grace is upstairs."

James shook his head.

"No, Your Grace, her went out 'bout ten minutes ago."

The Duke stared at him incredulously.

"Did you say," he asked, speaking slowly and clearly, "that Her Grace left the house?"

"Yes, Your Grace."

"Alone?"

"Yes, Your Grace."

"I cannot believe it!" the Duke exclaimed beneath his breath.

As he walked towards the door he asked:

"Did Her Grace say where she was going?"

"No, Your Grace."

The Duke considered this, until James said nervously, as if he was afraid he personally had done something wrong:

"Her Grace put on th' cape that were lying on the chair and told me to open th' door for her. I did ask Her Grace if she required a carriage."

"And she refused?"

"Yes, Your Grace."

The Duke could not understand it. Where could Honora possibly be going at this time of the night, and why?

Still speaking slowly so that James could not fail to understand what he wanted, he asked:

"When Her Grace left the house, did you see which way she went?"

"Yes, Your Grace."

"Tell me exactly what happened."

"I thinks it strange that Her Grace should be going out at this time of night, an' I watches as her walks out onto the pavement, stands for a moment, then crosses th' road almost as if Her Grace were trying to get into th' Park."

The footman glanced at the Duke, saw he was listening intently, and went on:

"I sees Her Grace stand for a moment looking through

th' railings. Then she walks down th' other side of the road an' I thinks to meself her were looking for a gate."

"The Park is closed at this hour of the night," the Duke said sharply.

"Yes, I knows that, Your Grace, but I somehow thinks, though I may be wrong, that Her Grace doesn't."

The Duke thought that was very likely. At the same time, why on earth should Honora want to go into the Park after dark, when it was crazy of her to be walking about alone?

"I am sure she has not gone far," he said almost as if he spoke to himself.

Then he walked out of the house and onto the pavement as Honora had done.

He stood there looking down the road, which now seemed to be deserted except for a carriage stopping at a house lower down which the Duke knew belonged to some friends.

It struck him that if they saw Honora walking about alone at this time of the night, they would think it extremely strange and would also question why he was standing on the pavement alone on his wedding-night.

Instinctively he stepped back so that he was in the shadows cast by his own house, and only when the carriage had driven away did he once again go out into the street, looking for Honora.

Now there was no sign of anybody, and although he stood there for some minutes, the whole place seemed quiet and deserted.

Because it was impossible for him to be inactive, he started to walk down Park Lane, hoping there might be some chance of seeing Honora.

Then he thought that if she wished to run away from him, she might have gone to her uncle's house in Grosvenor Square.

In which case, he reasoned, when she left the house she would have gone up Park Lane and not down.

He had no idea whether she had any close friends in London, but he could not help hoping that if she had, and had gone to them, they were not the sort of people who would talk.

He could imagine the news that she had run away from him would be a tit-bit of gossip that would sweep like wild-fire through the Social World.

That he, the most eligible and pursued bachelor in Mayfair, had lost his wife on the very day of their marriage would lose nothing in the telling.

He could almost hear the sniggers and the jokes that would be made about it.

He knew too that it would enhance the story if it was known that he was tramping the streets looking for his reluctant bride, and he would look a complete fool.

"How in God's name could she do anything so reprehensible?" he asked himself savagely.

As he spoke he turned and walked quickly back to the house.

James was still standing in the open doorway, and as the Duke walked past him he said:

"I imagine Her Grace will be returning shortly. When she does so, inform me at once. I shall be in the Sitting-Room."

"Very good, Your Grace."

The Duke walked back to the room in which they had been earlier and automatically went to the grog-tray in the corner.

But when he reached it he found he had no desire to drink, and instead pulled back the curtains to look out onto the garden at the back of the house.

There was a moon, which with the stars gave enough light to see the great trees that had been planted in his grandfather's time, and the flower-beds which in the day-time were a riot of colour.

But the Duke was worrying about Honora, and now for the first time he was thinking of how young she was and how inexperienced.

After all, she had said tonight that she had been in Florence for the last two years, and he supposed it had never occurred to her that she should not go out alone in London, especially after dinner.

He tried to remember if she was wearing any jewellery, thinking that if she was, it might attract thieves.

Because the idea of her being attacked made him nervous, he walked across the room and opened the door which he had shut when he entered it, so that he could hear anything that happened in the Hall.

He would know at once when Honora returned.

"I must make it clear to her that this sort of thing must never happen again," he told himself.

Then insidiously, as if somebody were whispering in his ear, he began to realise that there were other dangers she might encounter besides thieves.

She was lovely in her own way and, he suspected, very innocent. Suppose a man spoke to her? Would she know what to do?

Because the idea really perturbed him, he thought perhaps he should send for the Police to look for her, but once again he knew that there was no more certain way of inviting the scandal he dreaded.

However much he admonished the Policemen not to talk, he was quite sure they would know him as a sportsman besides being a Duke and a householder and would be unable to keep such a dramatic search a secret.

"What can I do?" the Duke asked himself, and thought that never in his whole life had he felt so helpless.

"There must be something!" he insisted.

There was no answer except to wait and hope that Honora would return unaware of the commotion she had caused.

Because he could not help himself, the Duke went again to the front door.

After looking up and down the road again, he walked a little way down Park Lane, only to see no sign of anybody except a prostitute in the distance.

As she was walking towards him and he had no wish to be accosted by such a creature, he turned and walked quickly back into the house.

He did not speak to James and once again went back to the Sitting-Room, thinking despairingly that in a little while there would be no point in waiting for her.

After that he could only hope that in the morning Honora would return from wherever she was staying.

He tried to convince himself that she had gone to someone she knew, and again he considered going to Grosvenor Square just in case she had reached her uncle's house by one of the streets leading off Park Lane.

But he could imagine nothing more humiliating than rousing the Langstone household, which would be asleep by this time, to ask if they had any news of his wife.

"I cannot do that, but what can I do?" he asked, and once again there was no answer.

Just when he was feeling that the only sensible thing was to make some pretence of going to bed, he heard James's voice and knew he was speaking to somebody at the front door.

He went quickly into the Hall and saw that the footman was talking to a man who was handing him some pieces of paper.

He walked up to them.

"What is it? What do you want?" he asked.

At the sharp voice of authority the man looked up at him nervously, but at the same time there was an almost jaunty note in his voice as he replied:

"If yer be th' Duke o' Tynemouth, I've brought yer two letters."

The way he spoke, rather than what he said, made the Duke certain that this in some way concerned Honora.

Without saying anything he took the letters James was holding, and, moving a little way into the Hall where the chandelier afforded him more light, he opened one of them.

He saw that it was from Honora, and before he read it he said sharply:

"Tell that man to wait!"

"You'd better come inside," James said to him.

The man stepped back before he replied:

"I'll be waitin' out 'ere, an' if 'is Nibs don't agree, I'll be orf!"

The Duke ignored what he said and started reading what Honora had written to him.

His lips tightened as he did so.

Then he opened the other letter, which was in a different handwriting.

It was, however, written on the same type of cheap paper as Honora's but in an uneducated hand, and there were several blots of ink on it.

He read:

> *Come alone with the messinger. If you talks to the Polise you'll nevar see your wife agan.*

The Duke read it through, then said to James:

"Order my carriage, and be quick about it! Tell the man who brought these letters to wait!"

James looked startled, then hurried to obey his orders.

The Duke did not stop to see that they were carried out but went from the Hall to his secretary's room in another part of the house.

He knew there was always a certain amount of money kept in the house in case he needed it, but he doubted if there was as much as five hundred pounds.

Only as he reached the room and lit the candle on his secretary's desk did he remember that as tomorrow was Friday, the money for the wages would have been drawn from the Bank.

The servants in the house were paid monthly, but the grooms and coachmen received their wages weekly.

As he found the key to the safe he opened it and found, as he expected, that there was money for his own use in notes of large denominations.

The wages for the outside staff had already been put neatly in piles ready for distribution the following day.

He counted them quickly and put them into a large envelope.

Together with the notes he always carried in his pocket,

and which were put there by his valet whatever he was wearing, he had just a little over five hundred pounds.

He closed the safe, blew out the candle, and walked back to the Hall.

He saw as he reached it that James had invited the messenger inside and he was standing against the door.

The Duke wondered if he had taken the opportunity to steal anything, then decided that would not be likely when the sum of five hundred pounds was to be handed over to him or his confederates.

"Who are you?" he asked.

"Oi ain't sayin' nothin'," the man replied surlily.

"I suppose you know the penalty for playing this sort of game?" the Duke asked.

The man did not reply, and the Duke thought that as he looked an inferior sort of creature, it was unlikely he was anything more than an underling to those who thought themselves in a strong enough position to demand five hundred pounds from him.

He therefore said nothing more but merely waited, feeling as he did so a growing fury and frustration at having to comply with what had been demanded from him by blackmail.

He actually waited only five minutes before there was the sound of carriage-wheels outside and James came hurrying back through the house to open the front door again.

But to the Duke it seemed more like five hours, and when he stepped into the carriage it was an added infuriation that he was forced to carry with him the messenger who had brought him the letters.

The man gave the coachman directions where to go in such a low voice that as the carriage moved off the Duke asked:

"I presume you are prepared to tell me where we are going?"

"Yer'll see when yer gets there," the man replied.

The way he spoke, with what the Duke recognised as a triumphant note in his voice, made him want to punch the man in the face or shake him until he received the answer he required.

Then he knew that the best thing he could do was to behave in a dignified manner, and he only hoped that when he reached his destination he would not find that it was some sort of trap in which he, as well as Honora, would find himself a prisoner.

Then he assured himself that it had all been done on the spur of the moment, resulting from Honora's foolish action in going out of the house alone.

As soon as the miscreants, whoever they were, received the five hundred pounds they had asked for, there would be no more difficulties.

However, he was not entirely optimistic, and when the horses came to a standstill, one glance at the house where they had stopped told the Duke where they were!

As he looked, he felt his anger rising furiously and knew it was going to be very difficult for him to hold his temper.

However, the sight of Kate made him take control of himself, and only when she had taken the money from him and counted it did he say in a voice that cracked like a whip:

"Now take me to my wife. One word to anybody about this, you understand, and I will have you closed down."

"You can trust me not t' talk, Dook," Kate said pertly, "an' the best thing for us both, as you well knows, is to part with no hard feelings."

Because what she said made a sort of common sense, the Duke did not reply but merely tightened his lips.

Kate walked jauntily ahead of him across the Hall to open the door of the room where Honora was waiting.

"Here she be, safe an' sound!" Kate exclaimed as she opened the door.

The Duke walked into the room and Honora rose shakily to her feet.

"You . . . have come!"

She was not certain whether she said the words aloud or whether they were merely a cry from her heart.

The Duke did not reply, he only offered her his arm.

Because she was trembling, she put her hand on it, then tightened her fingers as if to make certain he was there by holding on to him.

He drew her from the room, passed Kate in the Hall without speaking, and descended the steps outside to where the carriage was waiting.

Only when the Duke had helped Honora into it and was just about to follow her did Kate, standing in the lighted doorway, shout after him:

"Don't forget, Dook, always glad t' see you, if you've got nothin' better t' do!"

As she finished speaking she gave a loud laugh, and the sound of it seemed to flare out into the darkness of the night like the light over the doorway.

Then as the carriage drove off, she slammed the front door.

As the Duke sat down beside her, Honora was vividly conscious of his anger and knew it was what she had expected.

"I . . . I am . . . sorry."

"How can you have done anything so crazy, so insane, as to go out at night by yourself?" the Duke asked harshly.

Because of the uncompromising way he spoke and the agonies she had suffered while waiting, tears filled her eyes, and feeling that her voice was choked in her throat, she could not answer him.

She knew too that if she did manage to speak she would burst into tears, and feeling sure that he would hate a scene, she merely clenched her fingers together in an effort not to cry.

As if for the first time he was thinking of her rather than of himself and his own feelings, the Duke asked in a different tone:

"They did not hurt you?"

As he spoke he remembered that the impression he had had of her when he entered the gaudy pink bedroom was not only that she was very pale, her eyes seeming to fill her whole face, but that there also had been a red mark on her cheek.

Before Honora could reply, he asked:

"What happened to your face?"

"That . . . woman . . . struck me," she managed to answer. "She . . . asked me my . . . name, and when I . . . told her . . . she hit me because she did not believe . . . I was a . . . Duchess."

The Duke stiffened, thinking of the indignity of his wife being struck by a woman like Kate.

Then somewhat drily he said:

"But you managed to convince them."

"One of the . . . men had a . . . newspaper which . . . described our . . . wedding."

"That was lucky."

He suddenly realised what would have happened to Honora if she had not been able to convince Kate that she was married to a rich man.

He was well aware how many pretty young girls from the country disappeared in London when they arrived seeking work in respectable households.

By lies and other devious means they were enticed or kidnapped into bawdy-houses, after which there was no escape.

"Do you know what the place was to which you were taken?" he enquired.

There was a little pause before Honora said in a faltering tone:

"I thought it . . . must have been . . . a kind of . . . Play-House."

The Duke was surprised.

"Why should you think that?"

"There were . . . two girls there . . . and they were . . . painted as if they were . . . going on the stage . . . and . . ."

She paused.

"Go on."

"While one of them was talking to me, a gentleman, who she said was Lord Roxton, shouted for her."

"Roxton?" the Duke said sharply. "Did he see you?"

"No."

The Duke gave a sigh of relief before he asked:

"And you thought he had come to see a Play?"

"I heard him shout: 'I want Elsie! She gives a better performance than any of you!'"

The Duke was silent.

He found it incredible that anyone who had been in the brothel in which he had found Honora would not be aware what it was or the reason why the women were painted and dressed as Kate had been.

Then the indignity of knowing that his wife could have been at the mercy of such people and that he had been forced to pay an exorbitant sum to get her back made his rage sweep over him again uncontrollably, and he said angrily:

"I find it hard to believe that anybody could be such a fool!"

As he spoke, the horses came to a standstill outside Tynemouth House.

The footman jumped down from the box, and as he opened the door of the carriage the Duke saw that James was still standing waiting at the front door.

He alighted, and as Honora followed him he remembered to offer her his hand.

However, he let go of her hand as soon as they reached the steps and hurried up them into the Hall, leaving her to follow him.

Because his last remark brought tears to her eyes, she found it difficult to see the way.

Then as she stepped into the Hall she felt as if the staircase ahead of her and the lighted chandeliers over her head had begun to swim dizzily round her.

She stood indecisively, unable to move any farther, and put out her hand to feel blindly for something to hold on to.

She heard James exclaim:

"Is Your Grace all right?"

Then the floor seemed to rise up and cover her as somebody saved her from reaching the ground.

Then there was only darkness. . . .

* * *

The Duke, carrying Honora upstairs, was aware of how light she was, and as he looked down at her closed eyes and her head turned against his shoulder, he could see the vivid red mark left by Kate's hand.

She had dropped her cloak when she fell, and it struck him that she looked like a flower that had been buffeted about in a wild tempest and had its petals bruised by it.

It was not like him to have poetical thoughts, and as he carried her to the top of the staircase, then along to her bedroom, he suddenly felt ashamed of his anger against anything so small and fragile and, as he now knew, very inexperienced and incredibly innocent.

"This should not have happened," he blamed himself. "I should have prevented it."

As he reached the door of Honora's bedroom he saw that it was ajar and pushed it open with his foot and carried her inside.

As he did so, Emily, who had been sitting in a chair, waiting for her mistress, jumped to her feet.

"What's happened to Her Grace?"

"Your mistress has fainted."

He put Honora very gently down on the bed.

"Undress her and put her into bed," he said, "and I will get her something to drink."

"Oh, my poor lady!" Emily exclaimed. "Whatever made her faint?"

The Duke did not reply. He was relieved to learn that after he had left the house, James obviously had not talked to the other servants but had remained on duty in the Hall.

He went downstairs again, and as he passed the footman he said:

"I gather, James, you have not spoken to anybody about what happened this evening."

"No, Your Grace."

"I congratulate you on behaving in a most sensible

manner," the Duke said, "and I trust you to keep to yourself everything that occurred."

James flushed at his master's praise and replied:

"I'll say nothin', if them's Your Grace's wishes."

"They are," the Duke confirmed, "and I trust you, James, to keep quiet about all this."

"Very good, Your Grace," James replied.

The Duke left him and went to the Sitting-Room.

He hesitated for a moment, undecided whether to take Honora a glass of champagne or a glass of brandy, then decided that brandy would be the best.

He added a little water, then carrying the glass climbed the stairs slowly, thinking as he did so that it would be wise to give Emily time to get Honora undressed and into bed.

When he entered the room he saw Honora's gown lying over a chair. She was now in bed with her head resting against the pillows and her eyes still closed.

"Her Grace spoke to me," Emily said as the Duke reached the bed, "but I'm sure she still feels queer."

"I am sure she does," the Duke answered.

He slipped his arm behind Honora's head.

"I want you to drink a little of this," he said quietly. "It will make you feel better."

Honora's eye-lashes flickered, and as if she must obey him she took a tiny sip of the brandy from the glass he held against her lips.

Then as the fiery liquid burnt its way down her throat she made a little exclamation and tried to push the glass away.

"Drink a little more," the Duke said firmly, and knew she was feeling too weak to refuse to do as she was told.

He forced her to take several more sips, until as the colour came back into her cheeks he took the glass away and laid her back against the pillow.

She looked up at him, and as if she had forgotten what happened and was repeating what she had said before, he heard her murmur:

"I am . . . sorry . . . very . . . sorry . . ."

The Duke put the glass down on a table beside the bed and said to Honora:

"I am going to undress, then I am coming back to talk to you for a little while before you must go to sleep."

He did not wait for Honora to reply but said to Emily:

"Finish looking after your mistress, but leave the lights. I will put them out later."

Emily bobbed him a curtsey, and the Duke went through the communicating-door into his own room.

The brandy had made Honora feel that now the darkness was gone, and she was able to ask:

"What . . . happened? How did I . . . get here?"

"You fainted, Your Grace," Emily replied, "and His Grace carried you up the stairs."

"He must think I am a . . . nuisance."

"No, Your Grace. I thinks he were very perturbed. He tells me to undress you and went down to fetch some brandy."

Honora gave a little sigh.

She was thinking how angry it must have made the Duke when she had not only behaved in such a foolish manner but had also fainted when she returned.

She was sure he must have found it a terrible bore to carry her upstairs, and she remembered how her father had always said that men disliked scenes of any sort.

'I must tell him how sorry I am,' she thought, and felt miserably that already she had been a failure as a Duchess.

"I should never . . . never have married him!" she whispered.

Emily released her hair from the pins that held it in place, and it fell over her shoulders in curls on each side of her face.

She was wearing one of the fine lawn and lace nightgowns which her aunt had bought for her trousseau, and which, because they were a little revealing, made her blush when she first saw them.

Then she told herself comfortingly that nobody was likely to see them, and it was only now that she was glad she could pull the lace-edged sheet high up over her chest.

Emily finished tidying the room, then picked up Honora's gown and went to the door.

"Good-night, Your Grace, I hopes you sleep well," she said. "I won't call you early, until I finds out what time His Lordship wishes to leave."

"Thank you . . . Emily," Honora managed to say.

As she spoke she felt a sudden limpness come over her and she wished she could be alone in darkness and try to sleep.

Even as she thought it, the communicating-door between her room and the Duke's opened and he came in.

He was wearing a long, dark robe, making him seem even more impressive than he was usually, and almost instinctively Honora pressed herself back against the pillows as if she would shrink from him.

He looked down at her for a moment before he sat down on the side of the bed to say:

"I am not going to talk to you for long, Honora, because I think you must be very tired after all you have been through today."

Because she found it difficult to concentrate on what he was saying, Honora could only repeat what was in her mind.

"I . . . I am . . . sorry . . . very . . . sorry for being . . . such a . . . nuisance."

"I expect," the Duke said quietly, "nobody has ever warned you of the dangers there can be in going out into the streets of London alone at night."

"I . . . I realise now . . . it was very . . . stupid of me to . . . do so, but . . . I wanted to . . . think."

"What did you want to think about?"

He saw the colour come into her face and added:

"I suppose about me."

Honora nodded.

"Perhaps it would be wiser," he said, "if you told me what is puzzling you instead of trying to work it out for yourself, especially in the darkness outside."

Honora looked away from him and replied in a voice he could barely hear:

"I . . . I do not . . . think I can . . . do that."

"I think you should," the Duke advised. "After all, we are married, Honora, and it would be sensible not to have secrets from each other."

As he spoke, he thought what a hypocrite he was in that he had very many secrets which he hoped she would never know about.

Then he thrust these thoughts about himself to one side as he said:

"Trust me. I promise I will try to understand."

Because his voice was kinder than she had ever known it before, Honora replied:

"I-it was . . . something Aunt Aline said to me today and . . . which I did not . . . think would . . . h-happen."

"I do not understand."

"Aunt Aline said . . . the sooner I had a . . . baby . . . the better . . . and you . . . said when I . . . l-left you that you would . . . n-not be . . . long."

Although she spoke incoherently, the Duke understood.

"And that frightened you?" he asked.

"I . . . never thought . . . I never imagined, because we were being . . . married in such a . . . strange way . . . that you would . . . that we would have a . . . baby before we had even talked to each other."

The Duke was silent for a moment. Then he said:

"I must apologise to you, Honora. I see I have been very remiss, and I understand now exactly what you are feeling."

He saw a light come into her eyes, and she said, looking at him:

"Do you . . . really understand? And you are not . . . angry with me about it?"

Before he could reply she said:

"I know how much you have been . . . hating me . . . and I could feel it all the time we were being married . . . and because you hate me . . . I do not . . . want you to give me . . . a baby."

For the moment the Duke found it difficult to find words in which to answer her. Then he said:

"I want you to believe me, Honora, when I tell you it was not you I was hating but the fact that I had been forced to marry so precipitately in order to avoid, as I told you frankly, becoming the husband of Princess Sophie."

"I know it made you very . . . angry," Honora said, "but when I . . . tried not to agree to marry you . . . Aunt Aline made me . . . do so."

The Duke frowned.

"How did she make you do that?"

"She told me I must either marry you . . . or become a . . . Nun," Honora said simply.

"Do you mean that?"

Honora nodded.

"She said she would send me to the Convent of the Little Sisters of the Poor the . . . next day . . . and I knew it would be . . . wrong for me to take . . . the veil when I have no vocation to do so."

"It was a diabolical idea," the Duke said, "and you were right to refuse."

"So . . . even though I had no . . . wish to marry you," Honora said, "I . . . could not . . . escape."

She made a little sound that was very young and lost as she added:

"Because neither of us wished to be . . . married, and I know . . . how much you hated it . . . I am sure it would be . . . wrong for us to have a baby when it was not born . . . of love."

As the Duke found it impossible to find the right words in which to reply, Honora went on:

"When I was . . . small I remember somebody saying to Mama:

"'How beautiful your little girl is! I suppose that is why you called her "Honora."'"

"Mama smiled and replied:

"'As you are aware, "Honora" means "Beauty," and my

husband and I knew she would be beautiful because she was born of love.'

"The friend laughed and said:

"'That is certainly true. I have never known two people as much in love as you and your husband. It makes us all very envious.'"

Honora told the tale in a soft little voice. Then she said:

"I think . . . perhaps if we have a baby born in . . . hate it will be . . . ugly . . . or even . . . deformed."

The Duke drew in his breath.

Then he put out his hand and laid it over Honora's.

"I am sure what you are saying is unfounded," he said, "but I think, Honora, it would be wise for us to start again and get to know each other a little better before we think of starting a family."

He felt Honora's fingers tremble beneath his. Then she said:

"S-suppose we . . . never fall in love with each other . . . and you continue to . . . hate me?"

"I have already explained I was not hating you personally," the Duke replied. "If we both try to forget our wedding and what led up to it, perhaps we could play a game of pretending we had just met and both thought it would be interesting to get to know each other better."

Honora gave a tiny laugh that was somehow unsteady.

"I . . . I think that might be . . . rather exciting."

"Very well, then that is what we shall do," the Duke said, "but you must promise me three things."

"What . . . are they?"

"That you will not run away from me, that you will not go into danger as you did tonight, and that you will trust me and tell me what you are thinking and feeling."

He felt her fingers stiffen as if she was surprised. Then she said:

"Suppose what I am thinking . . . makes you angry?"

"I see no reason why anything you think should make me angry," the Duke said, "and shall I say I shall take a chance on it, and you must do the same?"

She gave him a little smile. Then she said:

"It might be very wonderful to be able to talk to you as I used to talk to Papa. Ever since he...died there has been nobody I could...really talk to about things that matter to me...and it has been...very lonely."

Because the way she spoke was very pathetic, the Duke's hand tightened on hers before he said:

"I shall look forward to our conversations, but now I think you should go to sleep without dreaming and without being afraid."

"I am...no longer afraid of you," Honora said, "at least...not at the moment."

"You are quite sure of that?"

"Quite sure, and I can sense that you are feeling... differently about me than you did before."

"I suppose, now that I think about it," the Duke said, "I can also sense what you are feeling. And I think, Honora, that just as you knew I would come and save you tonight, you know that I will always help you if I can, however difficult the problem may seem."

"Will you...really do that?" Honora asked. "I may be a terrible nuisance...and perhaps cost you...more money."

Unexpectedly the Duke said:

"Look at me, Honora!"

She turned her eyes to his, and he thought he had never before looked into eyes that were so clear, innocent, and unspoilt.

"What I want you to understand," he said very quietly, "is that where you and I are concerned money is not important, nor is anything else except that we must both try to understand each other and make our marriage a success."

His voice deepened as he went on:

"It may not be easy, but if we both try very hard, and trust each other, then I believe all the difficulties and problems will melt away."

As the Duke finished speaking, Honora's eyes were still fixed on his and he found it hard to look away.

He wondered if he should kiss her as he would have kissed any other woman in the same circumstances.

Then he thought she would not understand, and he was afraid of spoiling the vibrations between them and of making her afraid.

Instead, he smiled in a way that many women had found irresistible and rose from the bed.

"Go to sleep now, Honora," he said. "We will not leave early tomorrow morning, and if you are feeling too tired we can stay here for another day, but I am looking forward to showing you my horses."

"I want very much to see them," Honora said.

The Duke opened the communicating-door, then blew out the candles by her bed.

"Good-night, Honora!" he said. "Go to sleep quickly."

"I will . . . try," Honora said in a small voice, "and thank you for being . . . so kind."

She saw the Duke pause, and as he looked back at her she added:

"So . . . very kind and . . . understanding."

He shut the door, and she was alone.

Chapter Seven

There was the thunder of hoofs, and the horses raced neck and neck towards the end of the ride before their riders reined them in.

As they came to a standstill Honora cried:

"I think you won by one small, ugly little nose!"

The Duke laughed.

"Are you insulting me, or my horse?"

"I would hate to insult Warrior," Honora replied, "who has a soft, very lovable nose, while of course a Duke's nose is always disdainful and condescending."

"I cannot imagine why you should think that!" he exclaimed almost aggressively.

"As an alternative to being magnificent, omnipotent, and arrogant, it can also be cynical, supercilious, and of course bored."

The Duke laughed as if he could not help it. Then he said:

"I wonder if there is anything in the rules or in your vocabulary, Honora, which permits one to spank a Duchess!"

She gave a little chuckle before she said:

"You will have to catch her first!"

She touched her horse lightly with her spur and the next minute was riding wildly away from him through the Park towards the house.

It took the Duke a second or two to turn and follow her, and by that time Honora, riding superbly, had almost reached the gate which led into the garden.

Only as he caught up with her did she say breathlessly:

"I surrender, and I am quite prepared to say, if you prefer, that it was Warrior's nose which was in front."

"I will let you off this time," the Duke said mock-seriously, "but remember, there is one adjective you have not applied to Dukes, which is that they can be very revengeful."

Honora chuckled.

"I do not think you would ever be like that."

"Why not?" the Duke enquired curiously.

"Because you are not the revengeful type. I know you can be very angry . . . very angry . . . but you are not the sort of person to sulk and cogitate and plot how to gain your revenge."

The Duke smiled.

"Are you using your instinct, Honora, where I am concerned?"

"Of course," she replied. "How could I do anything else?"

She smiled at him as she spoke, and he thought he had never known anybody so unselfconscious or who seemed to so enjoy life every second she was living it.

When they had reached his Hunting Lodge in Leicester-shire for their honeymoon, the Duke soon realised that Honora was very different from what he had expected.

He had never imagined a woman could laugh so light-heartedly and find so many things amusing.

Honora's was not the rather artificial laughter of the sophisticated beauties with whom he had amused himself, who always laughed as if they were trying to remember to make it sound like a "peal of bells."

Instead, Honora's laughter came spontaneously and unaffectedly, and she laughed with her eyes as well as with her throat.

The Duke found to his surprise that the four days they had spent together so far of their honeymoon had been for him so different from any days he could remember that he could hardly credit his own enjoyment of them.

With Honora the Duke knew he had never laughed so much or been so amused by things which ordinarily were of no interest to him or else were too trivial to evoke a discussion.

He felt as if everything she said had a new meaning and, in some extraordinary way, had a funny side he had never known before.

When he rose in the morning he found himself looking forward to showing Honora another part of his Estate, deciding with her which horses they should ride, and answering the hundred questions she had for him on subjects that he had never previously discussed with anyone.

What was more, he felt as if she gave him a new appreciation of the countryside.

After living in Florence for two years, to her the country was like coming home to something very dear and familiar.

"Look at the green of that field!" she would exclaim suddenly. "Could anything be more beautiful? I only wish that after all I could paint."

"You must try to express it in music," the Duke said.

"It makes me wonder if hearing is as wonderful as seeing," she said reflectively. "If you had to make the choice, which would you choose to be—blind or deaf?"

It was the sort of question which the Duke had never been asked.

Because he was trying to keep to their pact that they should be entirely truthful with each other, he often had to hesitate and think before he gave her a reply.

Now as they rode through the gates into the garden and up towards the house, Honora said:

"I think this is the happiest day I have ever known!"

There was a rapt little note in her voice which the Duke did not miss, and he replied quietly:

"I have enjoyed it too."

They had set off quite early in the morning after breakfast to visit an outlying part of the Duke's Estate where there was a farm he wanted to inspect.

After they had done so, they rode beside a stream over the meadowland yellow with buttercups, and had a luncheon of bread and cheese at a black-and-white Inn situated on a Village Green.

They sat outside in the sunshine and drank home-brewed cider which the Duke warned Honora was very intoxicating.

"If you fall off your horse," he said, "I expect I can carry you back on mine."

"That would be very ignominious, and I am sure properly behaved Duchesses are never drunk."

"Certainly not!" the Duke agreed, and she laughed because he answered her so seriously.

She gave him a little glance from under her eye-lashes as she asked:

"Are you nervous that I might do anything to disgrace you?"

She was speaking without thinking.

Then she remembered that when she had been captured by the two men who had taken her to Kate, the Duke had been afraid that they might talk or that Lord Roxton might have seen her.

Because he knew what she was thinking, he said quickly:

"That is all forgotten, and the answer to your question is that I am quite sure, now that I know you, that you will be an exemplary Duchess."

Honora gave a little sigh.

"If only Mama were alive it would not be difficult, and Papa would have looked after me and prevented me from making any *faux pas*."

"That is my job," the Duke said.

"When we go . . . back to London you may find it very . . . boring to have a wife who keeps asking you . . . questions."

He could not help feeling it was something she had thought of before, and he said:

"I enjoy your questions, and that is the truth, but I am beginning to be afraid I shall not have an answer to them all."

"I am sure you will," Honora replied, "and shall I tell you it is every exciting for me to have a private Encyclopaedia all to myself?"

The Duke laughed. Then he said:

"While I think about it, I have an idea that that is the most flattering compliment I have ever received."

"I should have thought, as you have had so many, that you are blasé about them by now."

"I am just wondering," the Duke replied, "whether you are teasing me or shooting at me, Honora."

She gave a little chuckle which he thought was very attractive before she replied:

"You are much too grand for me to tease you, and I am definitely too frightened to shoot at you."

The Duke replied unexpectedly:

"When your face is in repose, Honora, you look like a small angel, but when you are talking to me there is a dimple that appears to be mischievous and a look in your eyes which has nothing at all to do with Heaven."

"If you are insinuating that I am a small devil," Honora replied, "I shall definitely be affronted. At the same time, I feel it would be more exciting than to be one of those snooty-nosed angels who sit perpetually round a sapphire sea, twanging a harp."

"I thought you were musical!" the Duke said quickly.

Honora laughed.

"You always have an answer. That is why it is such fun talking to you, as I am sure dozens and dozens of beautiful ladies have told you in the past."

The Duke wanted to say that while there had been quite a number of beautiful women, his relations with them could never have been described as "fun."

That was what he was enjoying with Honora, and now as they saw the house just ahead of them and the grooms waiting for the horses, he said:

"I think that after such a long day you should lie down before dinner, while I polish up my brain and think of new ways of confronting you."

"That is unfair," Honora objected. "You are trying to take a mean advantage. As it is, I feel a poor, crushed little ignoramus."

"Not a very apt description!" the Duke replied drily. "I will think of a better one by dinner-time."

He saw her dimple as she said:

"And I, of course, will have to lie awake deciding how best I can entertain my Lord and Master!"

The Duke did not answer because at that moment the grooms hurried to the horses' heads, and having dismounted he helped Honora from the saddle.

As he lifted her to the ground, he thought once again how light she was, and yet he was aware that she could handle the wildest and most obstreperous horse in a manner that he admired.

They walked up the steps side by side, and as they reached the front door Honora said:

"Thank you again for a lovely . . . lovely day."

She looked up at the Duke as she spoke, and he thought her eyes had captured the sunshine and that he had never seen a woman who looked so happy unless he had been making love to her.

When they went into the house, Honora started to climb the stairs while the Duke, having handed his hat, gloves, and whip to a footman, walked into the Library.

It was a very attractive room and the walls were covered with books except where there were some fine paintings of horses by Stubbs.

As he expected, there were a number of letters on his desk which had arrived by post after he and Honora had left that morning, and there were also the newspapers arranged neatly on a stool in front of the fireplace.

He glanced at the letters and decided they did not interest him and he would leave them until later.

Instead, he walked towards the newspapers, thinking that it had been a relief these past few days to be almost out of touch with both the Social and the Political World.

Then to his surprise he heard the door open and the Butler announce:

"The Countess of Langstone, Your Grace!"

For a moment the Duke was still. Then he put down the newspaper he had just picked up and turned.

Aline Langstone came sweeping into the room looking resplendent and very beautiful in a gown of pink silk covered with a pelisse in the same shade.

As the Butler closed the door, she held out both her hands and said in the caressing tone she always used when they were alone:

"Ulric, darling, I had to see you!"

The Duke ignored her outstretched hands and enquired: "What are you doing here, Aline?"

"I am on my way to stay with the Stillingtons," she replied, "and as I had virtually to pass your door, it gave me an excellent excuse to tell you how much, my dearest, I have been missing and longing for you."

The Duke was aware that in fact she had extended her journey by at least fifteen miles, and there was a hard expression in his eyes which she did not understand as he said:

"I think, Aline, it was most indiscreet of you, and if it becomes known that you have come here, it will doubtless give rise to a great deal of gossip."

The Countess shrugged her shoulders.

"If anybody hears of it, which is unlikely, I shall explain that I brought you some rather important wedding-presents, which actually you will find in the Hall, and George is not joining me at the Stillingtons' until tomorrow."

"I am on my honeymoon, Aline," the Duke replied, "and I think it was a great mistake for you to come here."

"Do not be so stuffy, darling," Aline said, moving a little closer to him. "I am here, and I want you to tell me that you are glad to see me and that you still love me."

She lifted her face to his, and there was no mistaking the expression in her eyes and the invitation on her lips.

However, the Duke made no response except to stare at her in a way that she found bewildering.

She did not know that at this moment he was suddenly finding, incredible though it seemed, that Aline Langstone no longer appealed to him either as a beautiful woman or as one he desired.

The Duke was used to his love-affairs, and there had been a great many of them, coming to an end slowly but inevitably.

But he had never known such an abrupt and absolute

finish to an *affaire de coeur,* what might almost be called a "fall of the curtain," as he felt at this moment.

He had been so easily aroused by the Countess in the past, and had thought that her beauty drew him not merely as a man but as a connoisseur, and he could hardly believe that at this moment she evoked no response in him whatsoever except one of irritation.

He was incensed that she should have followed him to the country and should dare to intrude in an unprecedented manner in the first few days of his honeymoon.

He was aware that if people heard of it, it would confirm any suspicions that had been in their minds before he married Honora.

Because Aline thought she knew how to cajole him when he was being difficult, she put her hands, palms downwards, on his shoulders and turned her face up to his in a manner which in the past he had always found irresistible.

The fire in her eyes, and her red lips parted slightly and waiting for his, had never failed to make him forget everything but her closeness, which could arouse him in a way no other woman had ever managed to do.

But now as the Duke looked down at her he felt nothing but an urgency to get her out of the house before Honora was aware of her arrival.

He remembered, almost as though it were being whispered in his ear, that she had confronted Honora with the choice of marrying him or of going into a Convent.

He could hardly believe it possible that any woman could have behaved in such a brutal manner, least of all one who had meant something in his life.

Almost as if it were one of the questions that Honora had asked him in the last few days, he heard a voice say:

"Is she a good or a bad woman?"

There was no need for him to think about it.

Aline was bad, and he knew now he should have been aware of it with the instinct which came first from his mind and then from his soul.

He stepped back, saying in the icy-cold voice he could use very effectively when he wished:

"I am not going to offer you any refreshment, Aline, as I think you should be on your way."

She stared at him in complete astonishment, and for a second or so her hands were still outstretched as they had been before he moved away.

Then she asked incredulously:

"Are you telling me, Ulric, that your feelings towards me have changed?"

"My dear Aline, must we have a *post-mortem* on the past?" the Duke enquired. "As you know only too well, I am now a married man, and it would be a great mistake for anything to spoil what I hope will always be a pleasant and friendly relationship between my wife's relatives and myself."

Aline gave a little scream before she said:

"How can you talk to me like that? Are you bewitched? What can have happened to change in just a few days what we felt for each other and the happiness we found together?"

"I think I have thanked you before for the 'happiness,' as you call it," the Duke said slowly, "and now, Aline, let me show you to your carriage. You have quite a distance to go before you reach the Stillingtons'."

He passed her before she could prevent him and walked towards the door.

She stood almost as if turned to stone before she put out one hand and said pleadingly:

"Ulric! Ulric!"

Her voice seemed to vibrate round the room, and the Duke paused, as if he was afraid that they might be overheard, although it was impossible.

His eyes were as hard as steel as he said:

"Pull yourself together, Aline. As we are both aware, servants talk and so do those who are in attendance on Her Majesty."

Because of the implication of what he was saying, the colour seeped into the Countess's face, but her eyes narrowed and her lips seemed to spit at him as she retorted:

"I understand what you are doing, Ulric, and I hate you, do you hear? I hate you!"

However, in view of what he had said, she had lowered her voice to little more than a whisper.

The Duke merely opened the door.

As he moved into the Hall there was nothing the Countess could do but follow him, and he said in a clear tone that could be overheard by the servants waiting at the front door:

"It was exceedingly kind of you to bring me these wedding-presents. As you say, they are of such importance that Honora and I will have to write immediately to offer thanks for them."

The Countess had reached his side by this time, and as they walked on together he continued:

"I am only sorry that you cannot wait to see Honora. We have only just come in from riding, and she is resting, but I know she will be very upset to have missed you."

They passed through the front door, and as they were going down the steps the Duke went on:

"Please give my best wishes to your husband, and of course we are both writing to thank him and you for the magnificent Reception you gave for our wedding."

As he finished speaking he raised the Countess's hand perfunctorily to his lips, then stood back to allow her footman to help her into her carriage.

The door was shut, the footman jumped up on the box, and the horses started off.

The Duke did not wait to see her go but walked quickly up the steps and back into the house.

Only as he reached the Library again did he feel as if he had fought a desperate battle in which he had been overwhelmingly victorious, but not without inflicting casualties.

* * *

The Duke seldom drank port, and after dinner he left the Dining-Room with Honora.

When they reached the Drawing-Room, the Butler poured a little brandy into a large glass and handed it to his master on a silver salver.

The Duke accepted it, and as the servant left the room he put it down on a side-table and said:

"I have something to suggest to you, Honora."

She had moved towards the piano and was intending to play it as she had the previous night.

Then she had played him a piece by Chopin and one by Schubert before he had said:

"Now play me something of your own."

"I . . . I feel rather shy at following the great masters. You are bound to think my work very . . . inferior."

"I think actually it will tell me a great number of things which you are too shy to tell me yourself," the Duke replied unexpectedly.

Honora looked at him in surprise before she said provocatively:

"Perhaps that would be a . . . mistake."

"I thought we were to have no secrets between us."

"Some things are too . . . secret to tell . . . anybody."

"Those are the ones I want to hear."

"Why?"

He hesitated for a moment before he answered:

"Play to me, and I will tell you afterwards."

"Now I shall certainly be very careful what my fingers say," she said with a smile.

He sat listening to her until she said:

"I think as I am a little tired I should go to bed."

"Yes, of course," the Duke agreed vaguely.

She had thought he was thinking of something else and did not like to ask him what it was, but she had wondered about it when she was in bed.

Now this evening she came from the piano towards him and said:

"You look serious."

"I am," the Duke replied.

Although she did not seem to be aware of it, she was looking very lovely in a gown of pale blue gauze.

It was the colour of the summer sky, but instead of being decorated conventionally with pink flowers, there were little bunches of small white rose-buds that were not yet in bloom.

It occurred to the Duke that they were in fact symbolic of Honora herself.

The few days that they had been alone had told him, as he had realised on their wedding-night, that she was not only very young and completely inexperienced but also innocent to the point where she did not even recognise evil, although undoubtedly her instinct could sense it.

It was this innocence which made him know that he wanted to protect her from women like Aline Langstone until he had awakened her gently to the realities of life that she would have to face sooner or later.

Because he was silent, Honora said in a small voice:

"What . . . is it? Have I done . . . something wrong?"

"No, of course not," the Duke answered.

He put out his hand and, taking hers, drew her down beside him on the sofa.

As he did so he felt a little tremor go through her, and his fingers tightened as he said:

"We have been very happy since we came here, Honora. I am therefore suggesting, unless you dislike the idea very much, that we should go somewhere where we can be even quieter than we are at the moment."

She looked at him in a puzzled way and he said:

"I am rather afraid that while we are here people will drop in to see us."

He saw a faint colour come into her cheeks, and she looked away from him as she said:

"I . . . heard that Aunt Aline came . . . here this evening but that . . . she did not . . . stay long."

"No, she came to leave some wedding-presents for which we have to write and thank immediately," the Duke said firmly.

"She . . . she did not want to . . . see me?"

"She had no time."

"I . . . I am . . . glad."

The words were spontaneous. Then Honora added:

"You may think it . . . wrong of me to say that . . . but this is such a happy house and I . . . I was afraid she might . . . spoil it."

"As I have no wish for her or for anybody else to do that," the Duke said, "I was wondering, Honora, if you could care to go to Scotland?"

He saw her look at him in surprise, and he explained:

"I have a house in the North of Sutherland, which I usually visit in August or September. It is quite comfortable although rather small, and you might think it isolated. But at this time of the year there are a lot of salmon in the river and the heather will be just coming into bloom."

He spoke a little apprehensively, then saw an expression of excitement on Honora's face as she exclaimed:

"I would love above all places to go to Scotland with you! Papa used to tell me how much he enjoyed being there, and it would be wonderful to see it with . . . you."

"Then we will go there immediately," the Duke said, "and certainly the most comfortable way to get there, and the quickest, will be by sea."

"That would be even more exciting," Honora agreed. "Oh, thank you for thinking of something so marvellous!"

The Duke did not relinquish her hand, and now as he held it in both of his he said:

"Did you mean it when you said just now that it would be wonderful to be in Scotland with *me*? Am I important to your happiness?"

"But of course you are!" Honora answered. "You have been . . . so kind and so . . . understanding these . . . last few days that I feel . . ."

She stopped as if she felt she was going to say something wrong, and the Duke said softly:

"I would like you to finish that sentence."

She shook her head. Then he said, still very quietly:

"Look at me, Honora!"

There was just a little pause before she obeyed him, and he knew that she was feeling shy.

Yet, at the same time, a little tremor he could feel

coming from her hands told him that, as if for the first time, she was conscious of him as a man.

"Shall I tell you something?" he asked, and his voice was very deep.

She was listening, her eyes on his, as he said:

"You tell me you have been happier these last days than you have ever been before, and I feel the same. I think what we have both been feeling, Honora, is the awakening of love!"

It was impossible for her to take her eyes from his, and as he saw the colour creeping up her cheeks almost like the dawn creeping up the sky, he thought it was the most beautiful thing he had ever seen.

Then as her fingers tightened on his and he knew she was finding it hard to breathe, he said:

"I love you, darling, but I have been afraid of telling you so in case I frightened you."

"I . . . I am not frightened," Honora said, "but . . . are you sure . . . really sure that you . . . do . . . love me?"

"I want you to tell me what you feel about me."

Her eye-lashes were dark against her pale skin, and it was impossible for her to look at him before she said in a hesitating little voice:

"Everything we . . . do is so perfect . . . so exciting . . . and at the same time . . . so thrilling . . . which is . . . something I have . . . never known before."

"And what do you think makes it different?"

For a moment he thought she would not tell him the truth. Then she said in a whisper:

"It is . . . because *you* are . . . there."

"My precious, that is exactly what I feel about you."

He moved towards her, putting out his arms to draw her closer to him.

As he felt her whole body quiver he knew that this was something he had never known before in the whole of his life.

He had never felt as if he held someone sacred close to him; someone whom he wanted to protect and look after forever.

He drew her closer and still closer. Then he said:

"You are sure, quite sure, that you are no longer afraid of me?"

"I love you!" Honora said. "I did not . . . know that love could be . . . like this."

"What is it like?" the Duke asked, his lips very close to hers.

"It is part of the sunshine . . . music . . . the loveliness of the flowers and trees . . . and of course . . . the sky," Honora whispered.

Her last words were almost incoherent, and he knew it was because she was wanting him to kiss her.

Then as his lips touched hers he knew that her softness, her sweetness, and her innocence were things he had never imagined he would find.

It was perfect and so very different from anything he had ever known before.

He kissed her gently, as if she was infinitely precious.

Then as her body seemed to melt into his and he knew that she surrendered herself, his lips became more possessive, more passionate.

When he raised his head he said softly:

"I love you, my precious, adorable little wife! Tell me what you feel about me."

"I . . . love you!" Honora said. "I love you until you . . . fill the whole world . . . and there is . . . nothing else but . . . you."

The Duke kissed her again.

"When did you . . . first know you . . . loved me?" Honora asked when she could speak.

"When I carried you upstairs after you fainted, I knew I wanted to protect you and never let you be in any danger again."

"And afterwards you were . . . so kind . . . and understanding."

"I thought you needed me, my precious."

"I . . . did."

"After that," the Duke went on, "I fell more and more in love every moment I was with you, and I can no longer keep it a secret."

"Please tell me . . . tell me . . . that you . . . love me."

The Duke kissed her until a little while later he pulled her to her feet, saying:

"Shall we go upstairs, my adorable one?"

He felt her draw in her breath, and he said quickly:

"I promise I will not do anything you do not wish me to do, but, darling, though kissing you is very, very wonderful, it is only the beginning of love, and I have so much more to teach you."

She hid her face against his neck before she said in a voice he could barely hear:

"I . . . want you to . . . teach me . . . I want you . . . now that you love me . . . to . . . give me a . . . baby."

"There is no hurry," the Duke said with a smile. "At the same time, my adorable little wife, I think if we do have one and it is born of our love, it will be very beautiful."

"Very . . . very beautiful!" Honora agreed. "Because everything I am . . . feeling, and I know you are feeling too, is so . . . exquisite and so . . . glorious that it could only have . . . come from . . . God."

As the Duke felt there was nothing he could say in words, he said it in kisses. At the same time, he knew that what she had said was true.

In the past there had always been a fiery desire leaping into flame between himself and a woman.

Yet, vaguely, although he had not put it into words, at the back of his mind he had known it was not real love—the love which the poets wrote about, the musicians composed, and the artists painted.

Now, as if for the first time, he understood all those things. He had found them, although it seemed incredible, in one small person who was still a child as yet unawakened to womanhood.

He knew as he kissed Honora that to awaken her from a bud into the full bloom of a flower would be the most exciting as well as the most marvellous thing he had ever done.

She was, he thought, what every man sought and longed for: a woman who was his own, untouched and unspoilt not only by other men but also by women.

She was his, and it was like having a perfectly clean sheet of paper in front of him on which he could write.

He thought what he wrote would be his contribution to life, which could be good or bad, according to the way he wrote.

The importance of his task made him for the moment feel afraid.

It flashed through his mind that he was ashamed of his past and the many things he had done which now seemed tawdry, second-rate, and unworthy of his own ideals.

Then he knew that just as he must make the future perfect for Honora, the past must not reach out to affect her in any way.

As he kissed her he prayed as he had not prayed for many years that he would not fail her.

"I love you!" Honora cried. "I love you . . . love you! You are everything I dreamt of and thought I had lost for ever . . . when I had to . . . marry you."

"Are you sorry or glad?" the Duke asked.

She gave the little chuckle that he loved.

"How can you ask such a . . . ridiculous question? Very . . . very glad!"

Then she gave a cry.

"Supposing because I was so afraid of you and you . . . hated me, I had become a . . . Nun?"

The Duke did not reply, he only kissed her fiercely and insistently, as if he was afraid of losing her and was making sure he had not done so.

Then, as if what they wanted was quite unnecessary to put into words, they moved towards the door and went up the stairs hand-in-hand.

When they reached Honora's bedroom they just looked at each other with a smile, and again without speaking each knew what the other wanted.

The Duke went to his room, where his valet was waiting, and Honora went to hers.

Because Emily thought she was tired and did not wish to talk, she undressed her quickly and in silence.

When the maid left her, Honora lay back in the large bed to wait for the communicating-door to open.

Now she felt a strange excitement which was like little shafts of sunlight seeping through her body and they seemed to move to music which was playing all round her.

It was part of the music she had already composed, but now there was a new melody sounding through it—a melody that was a paean of joy and wonder that seemed to reach towards the stars in the sky outside.

The door opened and the Duke came in.

Honora could feel the moment she saw how much he wanted her, how much he loved her, and yet at the same time she knew he was afraid of frightening her.

For a moment she felt almost protective towards him, and she held out her hands, saying:

"I was . . . waiting for . . . you."

The Duke shut the door and came towards her.

"That is what I hoped you sould say, my darling. Last night after you had played to me it was an agony I can never express not to come through the door and tell you how much I wanted you."

"Why . . . did you not . . . do so?"

"Because I thought it was too soon, and you would feel we had jumped too quickly from hating what we had to do to finding after all how very wonderful it was."

"It is very . . . very . . . wonderful for . . . me."

The Duke sat down on the bed and looked at her.

Because Honora felt a little shy, she asked after a moment:

"What . . . are you thinking?"

"I am wondering why you are different from any woman I have ever known before," he said. "You are beautiful, exquisitely beautiful, but it is not only that."

"Then . . . what is . . . it?"

"I think it is the goodness vibrating from you, and I have known very few good women."

Honora gave a little cry.

"That is a lovely thing to say to me, and I promise that I

will try very . . . very hard to be . . . good so that you will always be . . . proud of me."

The Duke put his arms round her, but he did not kiss her as she expected, but put his cheek against hers.

"If you are going to be good for me," he said, "then I must be good for you, and it is something you will have to help me to be."

"That will not be difficult," Honora said, "because love comes from God."

"I know," the Duke said, "but we have to live our lives on earth, my precious, and sometimes it is difficult to give love to people who are not lovable. Besides, there are always temptations and choices between good and bad."

As he spoke, he thought it was something he had never thought out before but now was very obvious.

In the past he had spent far too much time with what was intrinsically bad.

Now, almost as if it was a gift from Heaven, Honora had come into his life so pure, so good, so innocent, that he was afraid that what he had become and what he had done might spoil their happiness.

As if she knew what he was thinking, Honora put her arms round his neck and whispered:

"I love you, and because I can . . . feel what you are thinking . . . I know that . . . everything about you is . . . fine and . . . noble."

The Duke drew in his breath.

Then as if he had come down from the heights to which his thoughts had taken him his lips sought Honora's.

He kissed her until he felt her body move as if to music and knew that she wanted him as a man.

Slowly, as if still he was afraid to frighten her, he took off his robe and got into bed beside her.

Then as she moved into his arms and he held her closer and still closer, he knew that this was the love which would overcome all difficulties and sweep away everything that was wrong, wicked, and bad.

This was the love which Honora believed came from God, and it was theirs now and for all eternity.

"I love you, my precious, adorable one!" he said hoarsely.

Then as he kissed her and felt her heart beating against his, the sunshine, the music, and the flowers were with them as love carried them up into the glory of the sky.

ABOUT THE AUTHOR

BARBARA CARTLAND, the world's most famous romantic novelist, who is also an historian, playwright, lecturer, political speaker and television personality, has now written over 350 books and sold over 350 million books throughout the world.

She has also had many historical works published and has written four autobiographies as well as the biographies of her mother and that of her brother, Ronald Cartland, who was the first Member of Parliament to be killed in World War II. This book has a preface by Sir Winston Churchill and has just been republished with an introduction by Sir Arthur Bryant.

Love at the Helm, a novel written with the help and inspiration of the late Earl Mountbatten of Burma, Uncle of His Royal Highness Prince Philip, is being sold for the Mountbatten Memorial Trust.

In 1978, Miss Cartland sang an Album of Love Songs with the Royal Philharmonic Orchestra.

In 1976, by writing 21 books, she broke the world record and has continued for the following five years with 24, 20, 23, 24, and 24. She is in the *Guinness Book of World Records* as the currently top-selling authoress in the world.

She is unique in that she was #1 and #2 in the Dalton List of Bestsellers, and one week had four books in the top twenty.

In private life Barbara Cartland, who is a Dame of the Order of St. John of Jerusalem, Chairman of the St. John Council in Hertfordshire and Deputy President of the St. John Ambulance Brigade, has also fought for better conditions and salaries for midwives and nurses.

Barbara Cartland is deeply interested in vitamin therapy and is President of the British National Association for Health. Her book, *The Magic of Honey*, has sold throughout the world and is translated into many languages.

Her designs, *Decorating with Love*, are being sold all over the USA and the National Home Fashions League made her "Woman of Achievement" in 1981.

Barbara Cartland Romances (book of cartoons) has just been published and seventy-five newspapers in the United States and several countries in Europe carry the strip cartoons of her novels.

Barbara Cartland

The world's bestselling author of romantic fiction.
Her stories are always captivating tales of intrigue,
adventure and love.